PERISH
TWICE

ROBERT B. PARKER

PERISH
TWICE

WHEELER
PUBLISHING, INC.
ROCKLAND, MA

★ AN AMERICAN COMPANY ★

Published in Large Print by arrangement with G.P. Putnam's Sons, a
member of Penguin Putnam Inc., in the United States and Canada.

Wheeler Large Print Book Series.

Set in 16 pt Plantin.

Library of Congress Cataloging-in-Publication Data

Parker, Robert B., 1932–
    Perish twice / Robert B. Parker.
        p. (large print) cm.(Wheeler large print book series)
    ISBN 1-56895-992-3 (hardcover)
    1. Women private investigators—Massachusetts—Boston—Fiction.
2. Boston (Mass.)—Fiction. 3. Large type books.
I. Title. II. Series

[PS3566.A686P47   2000b]
813'.54—dc21   00-049963
                                                                      CIP

For Joan: I too favor fire

Some say the world will end in fire,
Some say in ice.
From what I've tasted of desire
I hold with those who favor fire.
But if it had to perish twice,
I think I know enough of hate
To say that for destruction Ice
Is also great
And would suffice.

— R O B E R T   F R O S T

CHAPTER

1

My sister Elizabeth came to see me.

Elizabeth is three years older than I am. We aren't close. We had spent too much of our childhood fighting over Daddy ever to be the kind of sisters that talk on the phone every day. To cement my conviction that Elizabeth was a pain, my dog, Rosie, didn't like her either. Since Rosie likes everyone, including armed intruders, it seemed clear that Elizabeth was special.

"What kind is she again?" Elizabeth said. "A Boston terrier?"

"Bull terrier," I said. "Rosie is a miniature bull terrier."

"I thought she was a Boston terrier."

"You want to see her papers," I said.

"Oh, aren't you funny," Elizabeth said.

We were having coffee at the counter in my kitchen without Rosie, who had left us and was on my bed at the other end of the loft, watching us carefully with one black eye.

"So what brings you to South Boston?" I said.

"Is this really South Boston?" Elizabeth said.

"The yuppie part," I said.

"Oh...this coffee is very good."

"Starbucks," I said.

"What is it?"

"Starbucks," I said. "This particular one is from Guatemala."

"Oh, write that down for me, will you?"

"Sure."

I wrote Starbucks Coffee on a piece of notepaper and gave it to her. She stuffed it into her purse. I waited. She sipped some coffee. I looked at Rosie. Rosie's tail stirred. But she didn't change her mind about staying on the bed.

"Do you ever see your ex-husband?" Elizabeth said.

"Richie and I see each other every Wednesday night."

"Do you do anything?"

"Do anything?'

"You know," Elizabeth said, "sex. It's all right to ask because I'm your big sister."

"Then I guess it's all right for me to say none of your business."

"Oh don't be so silly," Elizabeth said. "Do you date other men?"

"Yes."

"And?"

"Elizabeth, what the hell are we talking about here?"

"For God's sake, I'm just asking if you have sex."

"None of your business. Do I ask you about your sex life?"

"Oh, me, I'm an old married woman."

"Elizabeth, you're thirty-eight," I said.

"You know what I mean," Elizabeth said. "I'm just interested in what life is like when you can't stay married."

I got up and walked down the length of my loft, breathing deeply and carefully. I bent down and gave Rosie a kiss on the nose, and breathed some more and walked slowly back.

"We who can't stay married prefer to keep our sex lives to ourselves," I said.

"Oh, Sunny, honestly you're so quaint sometimes."

"Quaint," I said.

The sun was almost straight up and it shone strongly through my skylight onto one of my paintings that stood unfinished on its easel.

"You're still painting," Elizabeth said.

"Yes."

"Does anyone ever buy one of your paintings?"

"Occasionally."

"Really?"

I nodded.

We sat quietly for a while. Elizabeth reached over and got the pot and poured herself some more coffee. She didn't replace the pot. Just set it down on the counter near her where it would grow cold. It took some will, but I didn't reach across and replace it. I didn't want any more anyway.

"How's Hal," I said.

She carefully poured some milk into her coffee and stirred in two sugars, and put the spoon down and sipped from the cup.

"I think he's cheating on me," Elizabeth said.

"Hal?"

"Yes. I think so, and, isn't this funny, I want you to see if you can find out for sure."

"Me?"

"You are being a detective these days, aren't you?"

"Yes, of course, but..."

"I wouldn't want to hire some stranger," Elizabeth said.

"You want me to tail him? Get pictures? Catch him in the act? That sort of thing?"

"Yes."

"Why don't you just ask him?"

"Ask him? Don't be ridiculous. Why in God's name would he tell me?"

"Because you asked," I said.

"No. I'm not asking that bastard anything. I am going to catch him."

"You don't want to maybe talk about this with him, see about professional help?"

"A shrink? They're all crazy. It's why they became shrinks."

"Maybe not every one of them," I said.

"And most of them are Jews."

"Maybe not every one of them," I said.

"I don't want to discuss this anymore. Will you help me?"

"Of course. I was just trying to see if we could agree on the kind of help you needed."

"Well it's certainly not some crazy Jew," Elizabeth said.

I thought about going down and lying on the bed with Rosie. Arguing with Elizabeth was

4

futile. She was, as my father used to say about our mother, often wrong, but never uncertain. And like our mother she simply dug in deeper when her convictions were questioned. If they were actually disproved, she was entrenched for life.

"I'll do whatever I can," I said.

CHAPTER

2

Eᴌɪᴢᴀʙᴇᴛʜ ʜᴀᴅ ɢʀᴀᴅᴜᴀᴛᴇᴅ from Mount Holyoke and never recovered. It was where she'd learn to speak in that honkish WASP whine that she now found natural. And the fact that she had a Seven Sisters degree required her to marry an Ivy League guy. At twenty-one years and three months, in the summer after she graduated, she married a Dartmouth graduate named Hal Reagan, lived with him in the Back Bay while he went to Harvard Law School, and moved with him to Weston when he joined a downtown law firm, Cone, Oakes and Baldwin. He was now a partner, and at thirty-nine his prospects were bright and shiny. Or at least brighter and shinier than mine appeared to be.

My first decision was about my gun. It wasn't a big one, a S&W .38 special with a two-inch barrel, and mostly I wore it on a belt, under a coat, so I could get to it quickly. On the other hand I didn't expect a shoot-out with Hal, and since it was a glamorous October day with the sun gleaming and the temperature around seventy, I didn't want to wear a coat. But I had been a cop and was now a private detective, and since I had been responsible for discomfiting some mean people, I had promised myself that I would never go without a gun. So I compromised, and plopped the .38 into my handbag, along with face maintenance and a few stray bills.

Rosie's leash hung by the front door of my loft. When she saw me put the gun in my purse, she went immediately to the front door and stared bulletlike at her leash. I had no intention of taking her. It was hard enough to tail your own brother-in-law without bringing along a dog who, while beautiful, was, well, unusual-looking, and immediately recognizable. I would simply give her a cookie, pat her head, say bye-bye, and she'd be fine. Probably sleep on my bed much of the day. I slung my purse over my shoulder, firm in my resolve.

All my reading of Nancy Drew had left me with no real tips on tailing your sister's husband. Hal would recognize me the minute he saw me. My first step was to try it from a car, where maybe he wouldn't spot me. Which was why I was idling next to a hydrant across the street from the exit of the parking garage underneath the Cone Oakes offices on State Street. One of Hal's partner perks was a free parking slot there, and if he was cheating on Elizabeth, he'd probably have to drive somewhere to do it. I wasn't sure he was cheating on Elizabeth, and Elizabeth's convictions on almost anything were so ill founded that I had very little confidence in this one. On the other hand if you were married to Elizabeth, why wouldn't you cheat on her.

Rosie was in the passenger seat, staring out the side window, alert for the appearance of a strange dog at whom she could gargle ferociously. Sometimes my resolve is a little shaky.

At five after twelve Hal's silver-gray Lexus appeared in the exit slot. I had his license number from Elizabeth. He slipped his access card into the slot, the barrier rose, he drove out, and turned left onto State Street.

It was easier than it had any right to be. With me and Rosie behind him, Hal drove out of the city on the Mass Pike, and in a half hour we were in Weston.

"Maybe he's just going home," I said to Rosie.

But he wasn't. He turned off of the Post Road about two miles from where he and Elizabeth lived and pulled into the driveway of a big yellow colonial house. I drove on past and as I did I saw the door of the two-car garage roll up and Hal's Lexus drive into the empty slot next to what looked in a fast glance like a green Miata. Around a bend, I U-turned and parked as far around the bend as I could and still be able to see the house.

"If it's a client," I said to Rosie, "he wouldn't have a garage door opener and he wouldn't park in there and close the door behind him."

Rosie showed no sign of disagreeing. On the other hand, she showed no sign of hearing me either. She was intent at the side window. If a dog didn't pass, maybe there'd be a squirrel and Rosie could throw herself about in the car snarling and barking and snorting.

"I should catch them in the act," I said. "Get a picture."

Rosie remained on squirrel alert.

Hal had every reason to be a jerk. He was a rich kid, an only child of indulgent parents. He'd gone to Dartmouth and Harvard, and had become, at an early age, a partner in the city's biggest law firm. Inexplicably, however, Hal wasn't a jerk. I kind of liked him and had always wondered why he'd married Elizabeth.

"No," I said.

Rosie looked at me startled.

"Not you, my little petunia," I said. "I'm saying no to myself."

If Rosie could have shrugged, she would have.

I stayed put and at about twenty to four, the garage door rolled up and Hal's Lexus backed down the driveway and pulled away. I let him go. When he was out of sight I drove down and pulled into the driveway, cracked all the windows so Rosie would have enough air, got out, locked the car, walked to the front door. The sign on the mailbox said Simpson. I rang the bell.

After maybe two minutes, which is a long time if you're waiting at a front door, a woman opened the door wearing jeans and a white shirt. The tails of the shirt were hanging out. She was barefoot and without makeup. Her hair looked as if an attempt had been made at it, but not an extended one.

"Are you Nancy Simpson?" I said.

"Yes."

"My name is Sunny Randall," I said, and gave her one of my cards. "I'm a detective. I'm also Hal Reagan's sister-in-law."

The woman took my card and looked at it without reading it.

"Hal Reagan?" she said.

"Yes. He just left."

"I don't wish to talk with you anymore," Nancy said and closed the door.

I didn't contest the issue.

CHAPTER

3

I WAS BACK in my loft again, filling in a little of the background on my current painting, when my doorbell rang and Hal Reagan came up.

"Sunny," he said. "What the hell's going on?"

"You've spoken with Nancy," I said.

"Did you follow me out there?"

"Yes."

Rosie rushed down from her place on my bed and capered about. Hal reached down to pat her, but there was no resolve in it. He was obviously thinking of other things.

"You got a drink?" he said.

"Of course."

"Bourbon—rocks."

I made it for him and poured myself a glass of wine. We sat at the kitchen counter.

"She's a client, Sunny."

"No, Hal, she's not. You know it and I know it."

"You can't prove she's anything more."

"I can," I said. "It is only a matter of time and persistence."

He drank some of his bourbon.

"Did Elizabeth put you up to this?"

"Yes."

Hal had played lacrosse at Dartmouth and still looked athletic. His hair was beginning to recede, and his short haircut made no effort to hide the fact. I liked that about him. His suit was expensive. His cologne was good. He wore a Rolex watch.

"Why'd you speak to Nancy?" Hal said.

"I had to establish there was a woman there. I knew when I told her who I was she'd call you and you'd come by."

"And she did, and I did," Hal said. "You told Elizabeth."

"No."

"Why not?'

"I wanted to hear what you had to say."

"Does it matter?"

"If it didn't, I wouldn't wait to hear it," I said.

"You know Elizabeth," Hal said.

"All my life."

"Would you want to be married to her?"

"No. It's one of several reasons I didn't marry her."

"And I did."

"And you did."

Hal took in some air, and let it out slowly.

"And I was wrong," he said.

"And?"

"And what?"

"And what about Nancy?"

"Ahh," Hal said.

"Ahh what?"

"I don't know what to say."

"Well, is she someone you care about?"

"Yes."

"You could ask Elizabeth for a divorce."

"Oh God."

"You could move out and let your attorney serve the papers."

"I couldn't do that, Sunny. We've been married seventeen years."

"Or you could follow your present course, cheat on her in her hometown, two miles from her house, until she catches you."

"Which I guess she has."

"She thinks you're having an affair, but I'm the one who's caught you."

"But you'll tell her."

"I'm trying to decide that now," I said. "What would you like me to do?"

"I don't know."

"Do you like the status quo?"

"Christ, no," Hal said. "Why would I?"

"It allows you to punish your wife without leaving her."

"You think that's all Nancy is? A way to punish Elizabeth."

I shrugged.

"I care about Nancy," he said.

"Not enough to leave your wife."

"Well I can't just..."

"Why not."

He shook his head. I waited. He shook it again.

"It's just such a mountain to climb," he said.

"Swell," I said.

"I guess...you should do whatever it is you would do...if Elizabeth weren't your sister."

"This is what I would be doing," I said. "One of the charms of being self-employed is you can try to do the right thing whenever you want to."

Hal shook his head.

"Elizabeth couldn't say that," he said. "And if you said it, she wouldn't understand you."

I didn't comment. Rosie sat on the floor transfixed by the small but nevertheless real possibility that we might move from booze to food.

"She has probably never thought about doing the right thing in her life," Hal said. "Almost forty and still judges people by where they went to college."

"And quite harshly," I said.

"She is the queen of doesn't-get-it."

"I know."

"She can't like a painting unless some museum guide has told her it's good."

"Hal, I know Elizabeth's faults as well as you do. And I am ready to agree with you that they are numerous. But I don't want to sit here while you enumerate them, okay?"

"You don't even like her," Hal said.

"That's got nothing to do with it," I said. "Family is family."

He nodded slowly, less to me than to himself.

"I don't know what to do," he said.

"Are you prepared to go back home to Elizabeth and be monogamous?"

"No."

"Do you want some kind of counseling? I could ask Julie for a referral."

"No."

"Will you tell her you are leaving her?"

"I can't."

"We could tell her together," I said.

"How would we do that?"

"I could call her," I said, "ask her to come over."

"Jesus Christ," Hal said.

"Or I can simply report to Elizabeth what I have observed, and leave it to the two of you to work it out."

"We can't work it out. You know what she's like. For crissake, I don't even love her."

"I have laid out all your options, Hal. Either choose one, or I'll choose one for you."

"God, you're cold," Hal said, "like your old man."

"You wanted to get caught," I said. "You got caught. Now you have to do something."

Rosie stood up suddenly, and moved around my chair. The tension in our voices made her nervous. I reached down and she put her front paws on the stool rung and raised up on her back legs so I could pat her reassuringly. Hal breathed in and out audibly. I waited. He breathed some more. I waited some more. He took in a lot of air and breathed it out with a kind of a snort.

"Call her," he said. "Have her come over."

CHAPTER

4

WHEN ELIZABETH CAME into my loft and saw Hal there, her face tightened. Rosie had, of course, gone to the door with me, and when it turned out to be Elizabeth, had, out of habit, given a desultory tail wag. Elizabeth ignored her. Rosie seemed to expect no less, and went back down to the other end of the loft and got up on my bed.

"What's he doing here?" Elizabeth said.

"Visiting my sister-in-law," Hal said. "Something wrong with that?"

"Do you want any coffee?" I said.

"No. What's he doing here?"

"I have my report to make and I thought both of you should hear it."

"Report?"

"Yes. You asked me to investigate your husband. I did. I'm reporting the results."

"Well for God's sake did you catch him or not?"

I said, "Do you want to speak to that, Hal?"

Hal's hands were clasped on the countertop in front of him. He stared at them for a moment. Then he looked up and looked straight at Elizabeth and said, "She caught me."

"What do you mean?"

"She caught me. She found me with another woman."

Elizabeth took a step backwards.

"Who?" she said.

"No one you know."

"What were you doing?"

"Elizabeth, please."

Elizabeth sat down suddenly on a straight chair by the kitchen table. She began to cry.

"How could you do that to me," she said.

"For God's sake, Elizabeth, it's not just about you."

"Do you love her?"

"I..."

"Do you?"

"I don't know."

Elizabeth's hands were both clenched and resting in her lap. She began to pound them slowly against her thighs.

"Goddamn you," she said. "Goddamn you, goddamn you, goddamn you."

"Elizabeth, we have to talk."

She was crying hard now with her head down and her eyes squeezed almost shut. She pounded the tops of her thighs steadily.

"We have to talk," Hal said again.

Elizabeth shook her head.

"Elizabeth."

"Get away," she said. "Get away from me."

Hal was standing. He stared at her for a moment, then he shook his head.

"Fuck this," he said, and walked out of my loft.

Elizabeth looked up as he walked out and closed the door, and her sobbing escalated to a wail. At the far end of the room, on my bed, Rosie licked her nose nervously. I got off the counter stool and went and sat across the table from Elizabeth. I didn't know what to say. Elizabeth wailed some more. I wished I could feel sorrier for her. Maybe sibling rivalry runs deep. Or maybe there was something self-absorbed and annoying about her grief. I was sure that Richie and I had ended our marriage more gracefully. I waited quietly. After a while she stopped wailing and looked straight at me.

"Well," she said, "I suppose you love seeing your big sister humiliated."

"No," I said. "I don't."

"What's going to happen to me?" she said.

"You can probably control what happens to you," I said.

"Control? How can I control him? How can I control what other people do."

"You can control how you react," I said.

"Don't you goddamned lecture me, you couldn't hang on to your husband either."

"I'm not sure it's about hanging on," I said.

"Don't give me that crap. You and I both know where the bucks are, you want money, you find a man."

I looked down the room at Rosie. Now that the wailing had stopped, Rosie was stretched

18

out on her side with her eyes closed and her legs sticking out and the tip of her tongue showing. I envied her.

"Would you like to stay with me for a while?" I said.

"With you? Here? Where would I sleep?"

"The couch folds out," I said.

"The couch? Please."

"Just thought you might not want to be alone."

"That sonofabitch will not drive me out of my house," Elizabeth said.

I nodded.

"Elizabeth, when Richie and I broke up I found talking to a psychiatrist very helpful."

Elizabeth stood up suddenly and headed for the door.

"Well," she said, "I'm not you, thank God."

It was one of the few things we agreed on.

CHAPTER

5

IT WAS 11:05 in the morning, near Quincy
Market. I was at the very back table in Spike's
restaurant with Spike and a woman named Mary
Lou Goddard, to whom Spike had just introduced me. There was no one else in the restaurant. A lone waitress sat at a table against the
far wall, drinking coffee, smoking, and reading
Vogue. On the wall above her was one of the
several signs that said thank you for not
smoking.

"What about the waitress?" I said to Spike.

"Only need one until noon."

"She's smoking."

"Oh, you mean THANK YOU FOR NOT
SMOKING? That's just when there're customers."

"What are we?"

"Guests of the management," Spike said.
"Tell her your situation, Mary Lou."

Mary Lou was maybe fifty. She had short
graying hair and a square face. She wore a black
beret pulled down to her ears, and a black turtleneck sweater. She looked as if she had spent

her life smoking Gauloises and reading Proust. And enjoying neither. She eyed me as if she wasn't enjoying me too much.

"Don't worry how Sunny looks," Spike said to her. "It's her Meg Ryan disguise."

"Who's Meg Ryan," Mary Lou said.

Two couples came into the restaurant and stood hopefully at the hostess station by the door. One of the men had a 35mm camera slung over his shoulder in a black leather case.

"Excuse me," Spike said.

He stood and walked to the front and took four menus from the rack on the side of the hostess stand.

The guy with the camera said, "Four, for lunch."

"Do you have a reservation?" Spike said politely.

The man with the camera stared at the empty room.

"We need a reservation?"

"Always a wise idea," Spike said. "Give me a minute. I'll see what I can do."

He bustled around the room looking at tables and then went back and seated them at the first table near the door, put down the menus, and headed back to our table. When he passed the waitress, he tapped on the table. She nodded, sighed, dog-eared her page, put her cigarette out in her coffee cup, and went to take the orders.

"You tell her?" Spike said to Mary Lou when he sat down.

She shook her head.

"We were so entranced by the way you charmed those customers," I said, "neither of us could speak."

"I hate customers," Spike said. "Mary Lou needs some help."

"I can talk," Mary Lou said.

"Good to know," Spike said, and nodded toward me.

"I am the CEO of a organization called Great Strides. We consult from a feminist perspective."

"Could you tell me a little more about that," I said.

"Certainly. We consult to corporate America, identifying and suggesting solutions to issues of gender-based discrimination. We serve as a resource for law firms, and we provide research support for both the public and private sector."

"Girls R Us," I said.

Mary Lou looked at me stonily. Spike grinned.

"See, was I right how good you'd get along?" he said.

"I don't enjoy jokes," Mary Lou said. She looked down at Rosie noisily working on her soup bone. "Nor, I must say, do I particularly enjoy dogs."

"We can eliminate the jokes," I said. "The dog is family."

She nodded as if she expected no better.

"Someone is following me. Last week my offices were vandalized. A threatening message was left on my answering machine."

"Which said?"

"I would be killed. It was expressed in virulent sexist clichés."

"Was it a male voice?" I said.

Mary Lou looked startled.

"Of course," she said.

Rosie had stopped gnawing her bone and stood on her hind legs and put her forepaws on Spike's chair. He reached down and scooped her up and sat her on his lap. She sat with her mouth open and her tongue out and panted slightly.

Mary Lou said, "Spike, must you?"

Spike said, "Yep."

"And what would you like me to do?" I said.

"Protect me. Put a stop to the harassment."

"Why not the cops, get a restraining order."

"I don't wish to open up my personal life to public scrutiny."

"Then you know who this is," I said.

"What if I do?"

"Well, it is not something I do, but I probably could find a couple of guys to talk with the stalker forcefully."

"Spike has already suggested that," Mary Lou said. "I abhor violence and I will not be rescued by men."

In Spike's lap, Rosie turned and lapped his nose.

"I need a bodyguard," Mary Lou said. "Spike recommended you."

"I'm flattered," I said, "but I don't really have the resources."

"Money is not an issue."

"I'm glad," I said. "But I am essentially a one-woman shop. It takes more than me to do a first-rate security job."

"Couldn't you hire people?"

"Not women."

"I can't have men."

"There are men who will protect you without violating your consciousness," I said.

"I can't have men."

"Not even a tough fairy?" Spike said.

Mary Lou shook her head. Spike grinned. I sat quietly and didn't speak. Over the years I have found that a pretty good way to avoid being a dope.

"Can you help me?" Mary Lou said.

"I don't know how," I said. "One person can't do it right."

We all sat quietly. Rosie had stopped lapping Spike. She put her paws on the table, rested her chin on them, and began to snore lightly.

"I have no one else to ask," Mary Lou said finally.

I didn't like Mary Lou much. She had about her the same narrow certainty that my mother had. And she didn't think I was funny. And she didn't like Rosie.

"I have no one," she said.

Her voice was a little shaky.

"How is the security at your office?" I said.

"During the day it's good," she said. "There is a security guard in the lobby and my office staff is fifteen people."

"All women?"

"Of course."

"How about at home?"

"I live in a condominium in a secure building," she said.

"What floor?"

"Fifth."

"How tall is the building?"

"Ten stories."

I nodded.

"Can you help me?"

I sat and listened to myself breathe for a minute. I looked at Spike. He grinned.

"This is just foreplay," he said to Mary Lou. "She's much too softhearted to turn you down."

"Is he right?" Mary Lou said.

"Yes," I said.

CHAPTER

6

Julie, my friend since childhood, had a husband, a couple of kids, and an M.S.W. She did counseling and psychotherapy out of a small basement office in a house cum office building on Mt. Auburn Street in Cambridge, where she earned nearly as much money as she paid her nanny. Since my marriage to Richie had ended, Julie and I ate lunch together twice a week, usually on Tuesdays and Thursdays, usually at the Casablanca, sometimes at the Harvest, both of which were across the street and up a short alley from her office. We had started the practice when Richie and I had separated, probably because we both thought that she might be able to counsel me. We both recognized quite quickly that she couldn't, and got me to someone who could.

But we continued to meet, because we loved each other and because talking with another woman, whom you'd known all your life, is its own kind of therapy, even if I found myself more the therapist with Julie than the therapee.

Julie had a glass of white wine before lunch.

I had some Perrier. A drink in the middle of the day always made me sleepy.

"How's Richie?" Julie said.

"You know, that's always the first thing you ask me," I said.

"It's always the first thing on my mind," Julie said.

"But maybe not on mine," I said.

"No?"

I was silent. Julie smiled.

"Yes," she said.

"Richie's fine," I said.

"He seeing anyone?"

"I don't ask."

"For God's sake," Julie said, "that's inhuman."

"He doesn't ask either."

"Are you?" Julie said.

"Seeing anyone?"

"Yes."

"You'll be the first to know," I said.

"Sure you say that, but then you're sleeping with that policeman, Brian something, for weeks and you don't mention it to me."

"I forgot," I said.

"You see him anymore?"

I shook my head.

"He wanted more than I had to give," I said.

"Richie, still?"

"Yes."

"Maybe it's time to cut that cord."

"I think we have cut it. Now we are trying to see how else to be with each other."

"Jesus, Sunny, you are a persistent girl."

"Woman," I said.

Julie looked at me.

"Oh God, Sunny, you're not getting correct on me are you?"

"I've taken on a new client," I said. "She's a professional feminist. And she's raised my consciousness."

"A professional feminist?"

I told Julie about Mary Lou.

"Gee, send her to my house," Julie said.

"And send the bill to Michael?"

"Exactly," Julie said. "Is she a lesbian?"

"I don't know."

Julie ordered a second glass of wine.

"How does Spike know her?"

"How does Spike know anyone?" I said. "I think if I needed someone to play the flute for cobras Spike would know a guy."

"So how are you going to guard her by yourself?"

"Meet her at home, take her to work, leave her there, pick her up at the end of the day, bring her home, leave her there. If she needs to go out on business, or in the evening, she lets me know and I go with her."

"Do you think it's serious?" Julie said.

"I have to think it's serious," I said.

"Of course. But if it is serious, can you cover her by yourself?"

"No."

"Couldn't Richie find you someone?"

"They have to be women."

"And a good woman is hard to find?"

"A good woman who can shoot," I said.

"Ah," Julie said and drank some of her white wine. "There's the rub."

I hadn't seen Julie drink during the day. Normally she had patients in the afternoon.

"Everything all right with you?" I said.

"Sure," she said. "A little crazed maybe, but aren't we all."

"Kids?" I said. "Michael? Patients?"

Julie drank some more wine.

"The mothers of small children are all crazy," Julie said. "You know that."

"How about the fathers?"

"The husbands of mothers of small children are probably driven crazy by their wives," Julie said.

"You driving Michael crazy?"

"Sunny Randall, girl detective," Julie said. "I'm just playing with words, we're fine."

"Woman detective," I said.

Julie laughed. I laughed.

"You've got to be careful hanging around Great Strides, Inc.," Julie said. "Pretty soon you'll stop wearing makeup."

"Not on dates," I said.

CHAPTER

7

I WAS DRIVING a forest-green Subaru station wagon that year, and Rosie was sitting in it with me outside Mary Lou Goddard's condo in Chestnut Hill on a very nice November day when it was too cold and too leafless to be autumn anymore, but still bright and cheerful. I'd been there about two minutes when Mary Lou came out wearing a blue cloth coat and a white turtleneck sweater and big sunglasses. She didn't look as good as I did. I was wearing low boots and the latest in cropped pants, black, and a black sweater with a scoop neck and some nice silver jewelry. My revolver was in my purse. My hair was in place—or almost— naturally blond, and newly highlighted from the hairdresser. All around I had Mary Lou by a mile. She was carrying a briefcase with a shoulder strap and she looked like she was in a hurry. She went around to the passenger side and opened the door and found herself nose to nose with Rosie, who was sitting in the passenger seat. Mary Lou made a flapping motion with her hand.

"Shoo," she said. "Backseat, shoo."

I said, "Get in the back, Rosie," and she scooted over the armrest and into the backseat.

Mary Lou brushed off the front seat, and got in.

"I would prefer," she said, "that your dog not accompany you."

"She likes to ride," I said.

Mary Lou closed her door and we were off. Rosie stood with her forepaws on the armrest between the seats and her hind legs on the backseat, and looked out through the windshield at what there was to see. Mary Lou sat as far from her as she could in the passenger seat and frowned. Rosie ignored her.

"While you are in my employ," Mary Lou said, "I would prefer that you leave your dog at home."

I was scanning our surroundings, checking the rearviews, trying to see in all directions at the same time. If you're going to be a bodyguard, you can't operate on the assumption that there's no danger.

"Love me," I said, "love my dog."

"Are you saying if I employ you I have to put up with your dog?"

"Yes, ma'am."

She thought about it, and, apparently, came to some conclusion.

"Is that a rifle in the backseat?" she said.

"No. It's a shotgun."

"Isn't there a danger that your dog will make it shoot by mistake?"

"There's no round in the chamber," I said.

"I don't know what that means," Mary Lou said.

"There are shotgun shells in that tube there, under the barrel, but none are up in the chamber where they can be fired. In order to shoot, I pump one up by that wooden handle there near the front. That puts the shell in position and cocks the gun."

"So until you do that the gun is harmless."

"Pretty much."

"Do you have another gun?"

"Yes. I carry a revolver."

"You are carrying it now?"

"Yes."

A maroon Pontiac sedan had been behind us all the way since we left Mary Lou's place. In Brookline, at the light, I turned left up Chestnut Hill Avenue. The Pontiac kept going straight. I went up over the hill to Cleveland Circle and turned right onto Beacon Street, and headed into town that way. Nobody else made me nervous.

"Why did you choose to go this way?" Mary Lou said.

"I wanted to be sure no one was following us."

"Did you see someone."

"No. I'm just being careful."

Mary Lou nodded. I think she approved of careful.

"How did a young woman like you become a, ah, security person?"

"In fact, I'm a private detective," I said. "My

father was a policeman. I was on the force for a while and then decided to go private."

"A woman on the police force must have a difficult time," Mary Lou said.

"It's a pretty high-testosterone outfit, the cops, and I imagine there were judgments made about me based on gender rather than performance. But my problem wasn't gender. I just can't seem to work for anyone."

"Aren't you working for me?" Mary Lou said.

"No," I said. "I'm working for me."

"If that is so, how can I trust you?"

"Because I'm trustworthy."

Mary Lou stared at me for a while. Rosie was panting gently between us with her mouth open and her tongue out. She appeared to be smiling a big smile, but I suspected that was a matter of anthropomorphic projection.

At Harvard Street I picked up the Pontiac again. He was idling on a hydrant on Beacon Street, just past the intersection, and when I went by him he fell into line behind me. And he must have driven like hell when I turned off at Chestnut Hill Ave because Harvard Street is not a thoroughfare. He tagged me clumsily along Beacon Street all the way to Kenmore, where we crisscrossed onto Commonwealth and headed downtown. Maybe he wasn't clumsy. Maybe he wanted to be seen, so Mary Lou would know she was being followed. Then why had he let us go when I'd turned off Route 9? Maybe he was ambivalent. Maybe I didn't know all there was to know.

I could make out enough in the rearview

mirror to know that the driver was male, and to read his license plate numbers. Mary Lou did not appear to notice the Pontiac, and I saw no reason to mention it for now.

Mary Lou had her offices in Park Square. I pulled up in front of her building while Mary Lou got out of the car. Rosie immediately hopped into her place in the front seat. Mary Lou held the door open to talk to me, without a thought as to what might happen if Rosie hopped out and cavorted in the downtown traffic. I held Rosie's collar.

"I'll be here all day. You can pick me up at six."

"If your plans change," I said, "call my cell phone."

"My plans rarely change," Mary Lou said and closed the door.

The Pontiac had pulled in behind us halfway back down the block. I watched him in my rearview mirror as Mary Lou walked across the sidewalk. There was no sudden movement in the car. Mary Lou disappeared into her building. I picked up my car phone and dialed Marge Quinn, a woman I knew at the registry. She said she'd call me back in a few minutes. As I was hanging up, the Pontiac pulled away and drove down St. James Avenue. I followed him.

"See how this works," I said.

Rosie had slid down onto the floor in front of the passenger seat and was lying in a position that could not have been comfortable, snoring. Companionship. I was following the

34

Pontiac along Commonwealth Ave, going west, when my phone rang.

"Sunny? It's Marge. The car you asked me about is registered to Lawrence B. Reeves, in Cambridge."

She gave me an address on Brookline Street, which was, I knew, on the other side of the B.U. Bridge, near the river. In about ten minutes we were there, a two-family house, up and down, with yellow clapboard siding, and maroon-toned asphalt shingles on the roof. The Pontiac pulled into the driveway and parked. A middle-aged, middle-sized man carrying maybe a little too much weight got out wearing an ill-fitting double-breasted brown suit with a prominent chalk stripe. He was balding and what hair he had left was long and pulled back in a ponytail. He had on small round eyeglasses with gold wire frames. I pulled my Subaru up behind him, blocking the driveway. From the floor of the backseat I got my camera bag and took out a 35mm with a zoom lens and automatic everything.

"I'll be right back," I said to Rosie, and got out with my camera.

"Mr. Reeves," I said.

He looked at me as if I were carrying my head under my arm. I zoomed in on his face with my camera and snapped five pictures.

"My name's Sunny Randall," I said. "I'm a private detective."

He began to back away toward his house.

"Why are you taking my picture?" he said.

"You followed my car from Chestnut Hill to Park Square," I said.

35

"I don't know what you're talking about," he said. "Stop taking my picture."

He kept backing.

"You know what I'm talking about, Lawrence. You even let me lose you at Chestnut Hill Ave, and picked me up again at the corner of Harvard and Beacon."

"You're trespassing," he said.

He had reached his back door and was fumbling with his keys.

"We can talk here, Lawrence, in a friendly and open way, or I can come back with a couple of cops and we can talk in a more formal manner."

He stopped and turned toward me. His face was red.

"You bitch," he said.

"Ah," I said, "that's better. It's good to exchange ideas."

There was a rake leaning against the side of the house beside the door. He picked it up, still holding his keys in his left hand, his pinkie through the key ring.

"I'm going to smack you," he said.

"Gee," I said, "you don't look like a smack 'em kind of guy to me, Lawrence."

"That's the way you have to treat bitches," he said, and took a step toward me. "I like to smack bitches."

I have been threatened by a lot of people more formidable-looking than Lawrence B. Reeves; still, he probably weighed eighty pounds more than I did. And the rake might sting if he actually hit me with it. I glanced at my car; Rosie

36

was in the driver's seat, looking out the window at me. I dropped the camera in my coat pocket, and took my gun out and pointed it at him. He stared at the gun with his mouth partly open, and the tip of his tongue trembling on his lower lip.

"You're troubling my dog," I said.

"You've got a gun," he said.

"Yes, I do," I said. "And if you force me to, I'll shoot you with it."

He put the rake away from him. It fell onto the ground between us.

"Is it loaded?"

"Of course it is," I said. "Can't you see the noses of the bullets in the cylinder?"

"I'm going in now," he said.

He turned, fumbled the right key into the lock. I decided against shooting him for disobedience. It seemed counterproductive, and it might be against the law. He opened the door, went in, and shut it behind him. I heard the deadbolt turn. I went around front and up onto the front porch. There were two front doors. The one on the left had his name under the bell, Lawrence B. Reeves. I went back to my car and got in and exchanged kisses with Rosie, scooched her over to the passenger seat, and got in behind the wheel and sat for a little while in the driveway looking at the house.

If one had to have a stalker, Lawrence would be a good choice. He didn't seem too dangerous. Except that there was an ugly little salacious overtone tittering at the edge of his voice, when he spoke of smacking bitches. That was a little scary. It might be what had scared Mary Lou. I was pretty sure she knew who Lawrence was. Well, now I knew too. In a while I would know him better. I wondered why Mary Lou hadn't told me about him. While I sat, I picked up messages off my answering machine. There was one from Hal Reagan that sounded pretty desperate. I could go see him and then pick up Mary Lou and take her home. I was beginning to feel like Dr. Ruth.

CHAPTER

8

I STAYED ON the Cambridge side of the river heading downtown and crossed on the Longfellow Bridge. At three o'clock I was sitting in Hal's office at Conc Oakes, looking out the window at the coastline south of Boston. It was a lovely view, but access to it was limited to people willing to sit all day in a high office. Behind his desk Hal was in full uniform, white shirt with a pin collar, dark maroon tie with a small gold pattern, wide maroon suspenders. His cuff links gleamed in subdued self-satisfaction. His dark blue suit jacket hung neatly on a hanger on the back of his door. In his office, dressed for work, Hal seemed somehow complete. I'd never been to his office before. Mostly when I had seen him, at family functions, he was out of his natural context. Off duty, he seemed partial, as though he were in waiting. Here in his office he was larger, his clothes fit better, his smile was brighter, his eyes more piercing.

"Wow," I said, because I knew he wanted

to hear it, "with an office like this, do they pay you too?"

"Not enough," Hal said. "Want some coffee? Juice? Soft drink?"

"Coffee," I said. "Milk and sugar."

Hal leaned forward and spoke into a small intercom on his desk.

"Daisy," he said. "Two coffees for us, cream and sugar. Thanks."

He leaned back happily in his high-backed leather chair.

"How's Richie?" He said.

"He's good," I said.

"You see him much?"

"Once a week."

"Really?"

"Yep. How's Elizabeth?"

He shrugged. I waited. A sleek woman with her hair pulled tightly back came into Hal's office with a tray. She smiled, served us both coffee from a decanter, offered sugar and milk, put the tray on the side table in front of the window that opened onto the south coast, and left.

"You and Richie get along?"

"Very well," I said. "Far better than we did in the last days of our marriage."

"Do you think you'll get back together?"

"Depends," I said, "on what you mean. In some sense we are together. I think both of us know we'll always be in each other's lives. We're trying out various scenarios."

"Really?"

"Yes."

"Like what?"

"Like none of your business," I said. "I don't think you called me down here to chat about Richie."

"Now and then I forget how you are, Sunny." Hal smiled. "Thanks for reminding me."

"You want to talk about Elizabeth?" I said.

"Yes."

"Well," I said, "let's."

"Sunny, she's stalking me," Hal said.

I put my head back and stared up at Hal's elegant ceiling and breathed a little.

"Ah, yes," I said. "Big sister."

"She follows me when I'm with Nancy, she comes here sometimes and hangs around the lobby downstairs, by the elevators."

"Have you moved out of the house?" I said.

"Oh, hell yes."

"Move in with Nancy."

"Oh, hell no."

"I thought you cared about her."

"I thought I cared about Elizabeth once, too."

"Cautious is good," I said.

"So what are we going to do about Elizabeth?"

"What's this 'we,' paleface."

"Sunny, you have to help me."

"Hal, you are a partner in the biggest law firm in the city. Get a restraining order, get a divorce."

"I came out of Nancy's house two mornings ago, Sunny, and there was Elizabeth parked right behind my car. She didn't say a word, just sat there."

41

"Sneak," I said.

"You mean motels, under fake names, cash up front?"

"Yes."

"That's no way to live."

"Are divorce proceedings under way?" I said.

"I don't know."

"You don't know? Hal, with all due respect, you are a fucking lawyer. No *entendre* intended."

"I was going to let her get the divorce, I thought it was"—he shrugged, searching for the words—"the gentlemanly thing."

I stared at him.

He looked as uncomfortable as he was able to in his big office with his crisp white shirt and his cuff links.

"I... I don't know. I guess I'm feeling guilty," he said.

"So what do want me to do?"

"Could you talk to her?"

"I imagine so," I said.

"I mean, you got me into this..."

"Okay," I said. "I'll talk with her. But we both know who got you into this."

He nodded sadly.

"Thinking with my dick, I guess."

"I guess," I said.

CHAPTER

9

THE TIME CHANGE was in effect. It was dark early, and I was driving Mary Lou Goddard home from work. Rosie was in back, in graceful acceptance of her temporary displacement. Having had a look at the stalker, I decided there would be no need for the shotgun, which was home in my closet. So Rosie had the backseat to herself.

"Your stalker's name," I said, "is Lawrence B. Reeves. He lives on Brookline Street in Cambridge."

"You found him already?"

"Yes."

"What are you going to do?"

"Consult with you," I said.

"Did you speak to him?"

"Yes."

"What did he say?"

"He said he liked to smack bitches."

Mary Lou hunched her shoulders a little as if it were cold in the car.

"You know this guy," I said.

Mary Lou looked colder.

"No."

I was quiet. We were on the Mass Pike westbound, going very slowly when we went at all.

"You're sure about that?" I said.

"I am sure of whom I know and don't know."

"Last time I asked you," I said, "you were less adamant."

"I did not hire you to argue with me."

"Maybe just a quick fling, one night, somewhere?"

"Sunny, I'm a lesbian."

"Okay, so why is this guy stalking you?"

"Why do stalkers do what they do?" Mary Lou said. "I'm a public figure. Who knows what place I occupy in his psyche?"

"With all due respect to your prominence, Mary Lou, most public figures who are stalked like that are somewhat better known than you are."

"To the public at large, not necessarily to this man."

"Maybe," I said.

"Perhaps he is opposed to my politics."

"Well, no need to debate it," I said. "Sooner or later, I'll find out."

"No."

"No?"

"No. People like this thrive on attention. I think he should be left alone."

"And I can drive you back and forth to work for the rest of your life?"

"Perhaps he'll give up. Perhaps he already has. You may have scared him."

"Sure," I said. "That's probably it. Find somebody with a roaring obsessive compulsion, have a little straight talk with him, the compulsion goes right away."

"I want you to stay away from him," Mary Lou said.

I had spent too many years with my mother to think I was going to get anywhere with sweet reason.

"You're the boss," I said.

"Try to remember that," Mary Lou said.

"Sure," I said.

We were quiet for a while, eking along the turnpike.

"Have you a significant other?" I said.

I tried to change my tone, so it would sound like casual chitchat.

"I am with somebody."

"But you don't live together."

"No."

"Gee, I'd love to meet her sometime."

Mary Lou did a big audible sigh.

She said, "We are not in a social arrangement, Sunny. I employ you to protect me."

"Thanks for reminding me," I said.

We were quiet the rest of the slow way to her home. The minute Mary Lou got out, Rosie took her place in the passenger seat. I waited out front until Mary Lou was in the lobby, the door had clicked shut behind her, and the concierge was visible.

I said, "Mary Lou is lying to us, Rose."

Rosie didn't disagree.

CHAPTER

10

JULIE AND I met late in the afternoon at the bar at the Casablanca in Harvard Square. Julie had seen her last patient. It was Friday. And Julie was already into her second glass of Chardonnay. I had most of my first Merlot still left.

"Two stalkers," Julie said.

"One of them being my sister," I said.

"Did you know that I'm an only child?" Julie said.

"You get all the luck."

"So what are you going to do?"

"I thought I'd seek the advice of a professional therapist," I said.

"Like me," Julie said.

"Yes. What's your advice?"

"I don't give advice," Julie said. "I listen to you and say 'um hm.' "

"Well, let's talk about about Mary Lou's stalker."

"Um hm."

"Do you think she's lying about knowing him?"

"Um hm."

"Do you know why?"

"Un un."

"Thank God I've got you to talk with," I said.

Julie grinned. She drank the rest of her Chardonnay and gestured at the bartender.

"We know some things," she said. "We know that stalking is about power. The stalker gets a feeling of control out of it. You know, you watch them. They can't prevent it."

"I understand that."

"And I would guess, it's usually got a sexual base."

"That would be my guess," I said.

The bartender brought Julie another glass of wine.

"Keep in mind I'm not a psychiatrist," she said. "I have an M.S.W., and God knows I don't specialize in stalkers."

"Well, it's easy enough with Elizabeth," I said. "She's trying to keep some kind of control over Hal by following him around."

"And it works for her as revenge too. Obviously it is discomfiting to him and the woman he's bopping if the wife is sitting outside while they make the beast with two backs."

" 'Beast with two backs'?" I said. "Julie, you're so poetic."

"Shakespeare," she said.

"*Othello,*" I said.

Julie laughed. Her laugh was a little louder on her third glass of wine.

"One point for Randall," she said.

"Any thoughts on Lawrence B. Reeves?"

"The one who likes to smack bitches?"

"Or so he says."

"I'll bet she knows him," Julie said.

"She says she's a lesbian."

"Doesn't mean she doesn't know any men."

"Might mean there was no sexual basis."

"On her part, maybe," Julie said. "Not necessarily on his part."

"Good point," I said. "He can fantasize her as anything he wants."

"Or she could be more than one thing," Julie said.

I sipped my Merlot. The bartender pointed at Julie's glass. She nodded and he poured her another. Four.

"If she were bisexual," I said, "that would give me a lot more room to operate."

"Operate?"

"Figure out what's going on and resolve it."

"It would also double her chances of getting a date on Saturday night."

"Didn't Woody Allen say that?"

"He got it from me," Julie said.

She had begun to speak in that careful way people do when they are getting drunk and don't want you to notice.

"Maybe Mary Lou had an affair with this guy and broke it off," I said, "and he won't let go. Maybe this guy is just doing what Elizabeth is doing with Hal."

"So why won't Mary Lou tell you that?"

"She says she doesn't want her private life spilling out in public."

"Telling you isn't the same as spilling it out

in public," Julie said carefully. She had some trouble moving from the *g* in *telling* to the *y* in *you*.

"Maybe it undercuts her feminism," I said.

"A feminist doesn't have to be a lesbian," Julie said.

"Maybe Mary Lou doesn't know that," I said.

"Maybe she doesn't," Julie said.

She seemed to be losing interest in my professional problems. She was looking down the bar.

"What do you think of the guy in the brown tweed jacket with the longish hair?" she said.

"Wearing the scarf?" I said. "He seems a little languid, for my taste."

"You've always had this thing for butch guys," Julie said. "Didn't you learn your lesson with Richie?"

I'd never heard Julie criticize Richie before, nor imply any criticism of our relationship.

"I like a man who looks like he could change a tire," I said.

"Usually that's all they can do," Julie said.

"We a little mad at men tonight?" I said.

"It's the truth," Julie said.

"What's the truth?"

"Men are a pain in my ass," Julie said.

"Are you having trouble with Michael?" I said.

Julie made a pushing-away gesture with her left hand and shook her head.

"Oh," I said. "Well at least it's an interesting explanation."

Julie drank some Chardonnay and stared down the bar.

CHAPTER

11

MOST DAYS WHEN we went to the gym, Spike worked out in his karate suit. He didn't look like a karate person. He looked somewhat like a bear. I was in glossy coral tights in case someone might be glancing at me, and cutting-edge sneakers that went with the outfit. The gym was nearly empty, two or three trainers lounged around at the reception desk, and three women were running on treadmills. At the other end of the room, Spike was working on the heavy bag, and I was doing dips on the Gravitron, taking covert peeks now and then at myself in the mirror and being pleased that there was a little movement in the triceps as I pushed up. Strong girl. We talked sporadically as we paused to get our breath.

"What do you know about Mary Lou?" I said.

Spike went to the water fountain, took a long drink, and came back wiping his mouth on the back of his hand.

"Could you narrow the question at all?" Spike said.

"Let me tell you how things have gone

since I took her on," I said, "and you can comment."

Spike began to move around the heavy bag.

"Go ahead," he said.

I told him, while he hit the heavy bag with jabs, hooks, combinations. When I got through, he stepped back from the bag, gleaming with sweat, his chest heaving.

"Mary Lou is pretty certain about how everything should be," Spike said. "She thinks that she should be a lesbian. And she is a, ah, practicing lesbian. But she also seems attracted to men, and she thinks she shouldn't be."

"And does she give in to her attraction now and then?"

"I believe she does," Spike said.

"And how does that fit into her certainties?" I said.

Spike grinned.

"I don't know, but I'd bet—not well."

"Do you know any of the men in her life?"

"No. She keeps them pretty well undercover."

"Then how do you know?" I said.

Spike stared at me for a moment, and smiled widely.

"Sunny, it's me, Spike."

"Oh," I said, "that's how."

"Thank you," Spike said, and turned his attention back to the heavy bag.

"Does she have boyfriends that she doesn't bring into your company?" I said. "Or is it more random."

"Random, I think."

"You mean she like picks men up in bars or whatever?"

"More like that"—Spike did a series of karate punches to the bag—"like wham, bam, thank you, Sam."

I reset the Gravitron weight and did twelve pull-ups in necessary silence while Spike pursued the heavy bag relentlessly. I thought about Mary Lou's sex life to the extent that one can think of anything while doing pull-ups. And thought about it some more while I was doing the rest of my workout. When both of us were finished, we went and had some juice in the little lounge by the front desk.

"I like juice," I said.

"For breakfast," Spike said. "Right now I'd like maybe three Bloody Marys."

"Here?" I said. "That would be like fornicating in church."

"Probably why I want them," Spike said. "You got your sister straightened out?"

"God no," I said. "She's started stalking Hal."

"Lot of that going around," Spike said.

CHAPTER

12

I WAS HAVING lunch with Elizabeth in her house in Weston. I was never at ease in a place like Weston. The houses were too far apart. The front walks were too long. There were too many trees. The streets were far too empty, and I always felt as if a hostile savage might be lurking.

We were in her sunroom at a small table having pumpkin soup and a chicken Caesar salad, purchased for the occasion from the Fit as a Fiddle Gourmet Shoppe. Rosie wasn't with me. Elizabeth's home was much too spotless, and Rosie was certain to leave a black hair on a white surface, or vice versa, and I didn't want to have to fight with Elizabeth about that while I was fighting with her about stalking her estranged husband.

"Did Richie ever fool around?" Elizabeth said.

"Not that I know of."

"And now?"

"I don't know."

"Aren't you curious?"

"Sure, but I manage it."

"What do you mean, 'I *manage* it'?"

Elizabeth's scorn for anything she didn't understand was profound. There was a great deal that she didn't get, and if she accepted that, she might be forced to conclude that she was stupid. But inasmuch as she had graduated from Mount Holyoke, it wasn't possible that she was stupid. So I must be stupid. I understood it. I almost admired how well it worked for her.

"Divorce means that we both have the right to date anyone we wish."

"But don't you want to know?"

"Wanting to know doesn't do me or Richie or our relationship any good."

"Oh God, don't use that stupid word," Elizabeth said.

"Relationship?"

"God, I'm sick of hearing it."

"Okay, how about I call it friendship?"

"Friendship?"

"Yes, Richie and I are friends. We're working on whether or not we can be more than that."

"I would have thought that question was answered when you were divorced."

"I'm sure you would," I said. "But the divorce actually made the question possible."

Elizabeth laughed a nasty little dismissive laugh. It was a laugh I'd heard before. She laughed it when she didn't understand what was being discussed. It used to chill me into silence when I was small, and Mother thought Elizabeth was the smart one. It didn't chill me anymore.

"Hal came to see me," I said.

Elizabeth offered me some rolls from a small basket lined with a blue-and-white napkin. I took one.

"What did the slimy little prick want?"

I smiled.

"Hal's not so little," I said.

Elizabeth had put her spoon down on the table and was leaning forward.

"What did he want?" she said.

"He said you were stalking him. He wanted me to get you to stop."

"Stalking him? That bastard! I'll stalk him right into his grave. That sonofabitch."

"Why?"

"Why?" Elizabeth's eyes were shiny. "I'm not going to sit quietly back while he dumps me for some floozy. If he's going to keep fucking her, he's going to have to face me whenever he gets through."

"What's your goal?" I said.

"Goal?"

"Yes. What are you trying to accomplish?"

"What I said. I'm going to make both of them suffer."

I nodded and had some soup. It was pretty good.

"You tell our mother and father?" I said.

"No. Did you when your marriage went to hell?"

"Yes."

"And what did they say?"

"Mother said she was very disappointed and wished I had come to her before it was too late so she could have straightened us out."

"Oh God."

"Daddy said I was a grown woman, and would do what was in my best interests and do it well. If I needed anything I should let him know."

"He didn't disapprove?"

"Don't you know your own father?" I said. "He hasn't disapproved of anything either of us has done since we were born."

"Well I don't want you telling them."

"It's your story, you tell it when you want to," I said.

I finished my soup. Elizabeth cleared the soup dishes away and brought the salad. The sunroom buzzed of interior design. It was like an otherwise attractive woman in stage makeup. Everything was exaggerated, and decorative. I wondered how often she and Hal had sat here in the ornate sunroom in the elaborate house and talked about anything. It was hard for me to imagine talking about anything of substance with Elizabeth, yet Hal had dated her, married her, and lived an extended time with her. They must have had some sort of relationship.

"What is it you miss most about Hal?" I said.

"That's a dumb question," Elizabeth said.

"Give me a smart answer," I said. "Even it out."

"I'm going to get every dime he's got."

"You talked with a lawyer yet?"

"No."

"Who do you talk with?"

"I haven't talked with anybody. Why would I go around blabbing about this?"

"Elizabeth, there's nothing shameful about a marriage breaking up. It happens all the time."

"I don't remember you bragging about it," Elizabeth said.

I was remembering ever more clearly why I didn't spend much time chatting with my sister.

"The breakup isn't shameful," I said. "The thing is whether you go about it decently or not."

"Decent shmecent," Elizabeth said. "I'm going to make that bastard suffer."

"And yourself," I said.

"What?"

"What you're doing demeans you, Elizabeth. It allows him to govern your life. He goes out on a date. You have to follow. He doesn't go out. You can stay home. Who is in charge here?"

"That sonofabitch can't treat me this way," Elizabeth said, and her face began to clench and tears formed and she cried.

Oh shit!

CHAPTER

13

I WAS IN Mary Lou's office at 8:10 in the morning looking down at a dead woman. She had a bullet hole over her right eye and another one in her left cheek. Her head lay in a large pool of blood, which had soaked into the carpet and dried almost black. She seemed about Mary Lou's age, and when she was alive might have looked a little like Mary Lou.

"Should we call an ambulance?" Mary Lou said.

I shook my head.

"She's dead," I said.

"How can you tell for sure?" Mary Lou said.

"I can tell," I said. "Have you called the police?"

"No. As soon as you dropped me off, I came in and found her, and called you on your car phone."

"I was two blocks away," I said. "Who is she?"

"Gretchen Crane, my research assistant."

A silent uneasy group of women began to

gather outside the office door in the part of the office where most of them worked at desks without partitions. Several people carried paper cups of coffee. Which was what I had been on my way to get when Mary Lou had called me. I went to the phone and dialed police headquarters and asked for homicide and reported a murder.

In five minutes two uniforms arrived and told everybody to leave everything alone. In ten more two homicide detectives came by, accompanied by four crime-scene specialists, two EMTs, and a man from the coroner's office. Gretchen was pronounced dead. Yellow tape was strung, pictures were taken, a chalk outline was made around the body. One of the detectives began to question the women in the office. The other one, a detective named Farrell, talked with me, and with Mary Lou.

"The victim usually here this early?" Farrell said.

"She is usually here by six A.M.," Mary Lou said.

She sounded sort of annoyed, as if Farrell should know that and had no business asking.

"There's an empty carton that looks like it used to be Chinese food, on the desk," I said.

"I noticed that," Farrell said. "Some chopsticks on the floor under the desk."

"So maybe she was working late, having a little supper, and was killed last night."

"M.E. will tell us eventually," Farrell said. "You're Phil Randall's kid."

"Yes."

"You used to be on the job."

"For a bit."

"Phil's a stand-up guy," Farrell said.

"Do I need a lawyer," Mary Lou said.

It was as if she wanted to be part of the conversation.

"I don't know," Farrell said. "Do you?"

"I didn't kill her, if that's what you meant," Mary Lou said.

"So why would you need a lawyer?"

"The police are not usually very sympathetic," she said, "to sexual diversity."

"The victim was sexually diverse?"

"No, I was speaking of myself."

"You're sexually diverse?"

"Are you being deliberately obtuse?" Mary Lou said. "I'm a lesbian."

"Do you have any thoughts on who might have killed Ms. Crane?"

"No. None at all."

"You, Sunny?"

"Well, Ms. Goddard was being stalked."

"Sunny," Mary Lou said, "that's privileged communication."

"You and I have no privilege, Mary Lou."

"Everything I have said to you has been in confidence."

"Has it occurred to you yet that this was a mistake? That the victim was supposed to be you?"

"Me?"

"This woman bears some resemblance to you. She's in your office. It's in your best interest to talk about the stalker."

"This is a murder case, Ms. Goddard," Farrell said. "No secrets."

"I wish to call my attorney."

Farrell sighed.

"It's your phone," he said. "Sunny?"

"Sunny, you are not to reveal a single thing."

"This man may have murdered your friend," I said, nodding at the chalk-striped remains of Gretchen Crane.

"I don't know that," Mary Lou said. "When I do know who killed her, I'll decide what we will say."

"I can stall," I said, "but sooner or later I'll have to tell what I know."

"If you do so without my permission, you are fired."

"And if you don't," Farrell said smiling, "we'll yank your license."

"Give me a couple of days," I said to Farrell. "It is detrimental to my professional future if I get fired by a client for blabbing to the cops."

Farrell nodded and smiled.

"It's pretty detrimental to get your license pulled," he said.

"Give me a little room," I said.

Farrell nodded.

"I like your old man," he said. "You used to be on the job. Come see me tomorrow."

"That's as much room as you can give me?"

"That's a lot of room for somebody holding back the name of the prime suspect in a homicide."

Mary Lou was reading her Rolodex and dialing her lawyer.

"When you put it that way," I said, "I guess it is."

"So you'll be in tomorrow," he said.

"Yes," I said. "I will."

CHAPTER

14

THERE WERE STILL a couple of cops in the outer office when I sat in the inner office with Mary Lou and her lawyer, a small perky woman with a beaky nose who looked a little like a smart chicken. The lawyer's name was Rosalyn Gelb. It was nearly noon.

"First of all, Mary Lou," I said, "I am in an untenable position. I have no legal right to withhold information from the police, nor do I think I should."

"Had I wished the police to know my business, I would have gone straight to them. Whatever you know you found out while you were in my employ. The information belongs to me."

"I'm sure Ms. Gelb will tell you that your argument has no legal basis," I said.

Ms. Gelb nodded.

"New law is made all the time," Mary Lou said. "You do not have my permission to reveal any information you gathered on my time."

"Second of all," I said, "this is a murder investigation, and probably a high-profile one. Reputable white woman, associated with a prominent feminist, killed in her downtown office. They will want to kill this case. I know the homicide commander, Martin Quirk. If he thinks you are holding out on him in this case, he will tear your life apart."

"I expect Rosalyn to insulate me from that."

Ms. Gelb didn't look very happy.

"Third of all," I said, "why in hell don't you want me to tell them about Lawrence B. Reeves?"

"Because I don't," Mary Lou said.

"Is there anything you can tell me about him? Do you know him?"

Mary Lou sat in silence, her arms folded across her chest.

I looked at the lawyer.

Ms. Gelb said, "I'll do whatever I can to help you, Mary Lou. But I'm inclined to agree with Ms. Randall."

Mary Lou sat with her arms folded and her mind made up.

"Okay," I said. "I'll try to find a way around this, and if I can't I'll give you as much warning as possible."

"At which moment," Mary Lou said, "you are no longer employed by me."

I had nothing else to say. Apparently nobody else did either. After a long minute of silence I got up and walked out and went home.

When I got there, Rosie did her usual several spins and then ran to her water dish and drank half her body weight. When her glad-to-see-you ritual was done, and she would hold still long enough for me to hook the leash on her collar, I took her for a walk. We walked down Summer Street to the bridge over Fort Point Channel and stopped there. Rosie very much enjoyed looking down at the water, while I leaned on the bridge railing and fielded the inevitable questions about her species, gender, and purpose.

"Is that a pit bull?"

"No, she's a miniature bull terrier. She bears no resemblance to a pit bull."

What was going on with Lawrence B. Reeves? Why didn't Mary Lou want him named? Why was he stalking her? Why had he been so freaky when I confronted him?

"Is that a dog?"

"Yes."

She had to know him. It was the only thing that made sense. There would be no reason to conceal him if she didn't know him.

"Does he bite?"

"Depends. She's a wonderful ratter."

And she had to know him in a way that would somehow compromise her. A small child walked by, holding its mother's hand. Rosie barked at him.

The kid said, "Bad doggie."

The mother and I glared at each other.

The only thing I could think of was to look into Lawrence B. Reeves and see if I could backtrack him to Mary Lou. I looked down at the slick black surface of the water. It moved sluggishly. Rosie stared down at it through the fence railing, her tail wagging. I wasn't likely to find out very much about Lawrence B. Reeves by tomorrow and I knew Farrell wasn't bluffing. Whether he'd get my license lifted or not wasn't clear, but I knew he'd come after me if I didn't go in tomorrow; besides, I'd said I would. I had already decided, I realized, that I would have to tell Farrell what he wanted to know.

A panhandler stopped beside us.

"What a cute dog," the panhandler said. "Wha's his name."

"Fang," I said.

"Can I pat him?"

"Better not," I said. "He's vicious."

"You got any spare change?"

"No."

"Have a nice day," the panhandler said.

"You bet," I said.

The panhandler moved off. I looked at Rosie. Who was still focused on the glossy black water moving sluggishly below her.

"Mommy's in a foul mood," I said aloud.

Rosie ignored me.

"Want a cookie?" I said.

Rosie turned abruptly and stared straight up at me with her opaque little black eyes gleaming.

"Come on," I said, "we'll go home and get a cookie."

I turned from the railing and started back up Summer Street. Rosie trotted along in front of me with never a backward glance at the bridge.

CHAPTER

15

BACK IN MY loft, I gave Rosie her cookie, and called Mary Lou to announce my decision. The conversation was short, unpleasant, and ended, as promised, with me being fired. I left Rosie asleep on the bed with her feet sticking up, and went over to the new Police Headquarters Building. Lee Farrell was at his desk in the Homicide Bureau. There was a chair beside the desk. I sat in it.

"You're early," Farrell said. "Who's the stalker?"

I handed him one of the pictures I'd taken.

"His name is Lawrence B. Reeves," I said. "He lives on Brookline Street in Cambridge. I wrote the address on the back."

"Your, ah, employer know you've told me?"

"Yes."

"And?"

"I've been fired."

"Sorry about that," Farrell said, though not like he meant it much. "Why doesn't she want us know this guy's name?"

"I don't know."

"She know him?"

"I don't know."

"I'll go talk with him," Farrell said.

"May I come along?"

"I thought you were fired."

"Can I come along anyway?"

Farrell grinned.

"Nosy broad?" he said.

"Stubborn broad," I said.

"The best kind. You free now?"

"Completely."

"You're living that close to the edge?" Farrell said. "No other clients?"

"My brother-in-law, sort of."

Farrell shook his head. He looked at his watch.

"Four o'clock," he said. "I'll get someone from Cambridge to meet us there and we'll go see if he's home."

A Cambridge detective named Bernie Larkin was sitting in his car outside Lawrence B. Reeves's house when we arrived. Farrell introduced me.

"He's in there," Larkin said. "I saw him peeking out the front window when I parked."

"Okay, we're just here to talk with him," Farrell said as we walked up the front walk. "There shouldn't be any trouble."

"On the other hand he's a murder suspect," Larkin said.

Farrell unbuttoned his sport coat.

"So far," Farrell said.

Larkin took out his gun and held it by his side and stood to the left of the door. I had mine unholstered, holding it in the side pocket of my coat. Farrell rang the front door bell. Nothing. He rang it again. Footsteps. Then silence. Farrell rang a third time. The door opened slightly. It was on a chain bolt. A narrow part of Lawrence B. Reeves peered out.

"What do you want?"

Farrell held up his badge.

"My name is Detective Lee Farrell," he said. "Boston Police. This is Detective Bernie Larkin of the Cambridge Police. We need to talk with you."

"What about?"

"About a murder in the offices of Mary Lou Goddard."

"No."

"Mr. Reeves, we need to talk."

"No."

Farrell smiled.

"And," he said pleasantly, "we will. There's the civilized way, where you invite us in, and we chat pleasantly..."

"No. Go away."

"...or we can go the Wild West route, where Detective Larkin calls the station and some people come up and kick in your door and we arrest you."

The one eye that Reeves was looking out the door opening with shifted toward me. With my coat collar up, holding my gun in my coat pocket, I felt like Georgette Raft.

"She told you, didn't she?"

"Open the door, Lawrence."

"That bitch told you," he said. "I have to close the door to unhook the chain."

"Sure," Farrell said.

The door closed. Farrell put his hand on his gun butt under his jacket. I tensed. All three of us knew that when the door opened you could not be sure what would come out. I heard the chain rattle inside, then the door opened and Lawrence B. Reeves gestured us in.

We were in the downstairs hall of a two-family house. The stairs to the second floor ran up the right-hand wall. Glass double doors opened into a living room that ran narrowly along the left-hand side of the house. Reeves brought us in there. The room was not enticing. The furniture was shabby. There was a lot of dust, teacups with used tea bags drying in the bottom were here and there on surfaces that would hold them. A lot of newspapers, not all of them recent, were in a slovenly pile near the couch, which was obviously sprung, and covered with a multicolored crocheted throw. Farrell and I sat on the couch. Larkin, his gun out of sight again, was leaning in the doorway. Reeves sat in a straight chair with rounded arms and carved feet. He gazed at me balefully.

"You are Lawrence B. Reeves?" Farrell said.

"Yes. She told you, didn't she?"

"Where were you last night from, say, midnight to eight?"

"Mostly I was in bed."

"Can anyone testify to that?"

An odd look came into Lawrence's eyes.

"Maybe."

"Maybe?"

"Why do you want to know?"

"Well, we understand you were stalking Mary Lou Goddard," Farrell said.

Reeves glared at me some more.

"And," Farrell said, "we thought it would make sense to eliminate you as a murder suspect."

"Mary Lou wasn't killed."

"No, her assistant. We think it could be mistaken identity."

"Because this bitch says I was following Mary Lou, you think I killed her."

"The bitch rap is beginning to annoy me," Farrell said. "Do you have an alibi for last night."

"There was a woman here," Reeves said. He looked straight at me. "We came here from the Casablanca at 10:45 last night. She stayed until 9:30 this morning. We had breakfast together."

"Way to go, Lawrence," Larkin said from the doorway.

"There are a lot of women come here," Reeves said.

"What is this one's name?"

"I can't tell you her name."

"We'll need to verify the alibi, Lawrence."

"A gentleman does not kiss and tell."

Farrell took in some air through his nose and let it out slowly.

"A gentleman can get his ass kicked up between his ears," Farrell said.

"Police violence," Reeves said. "I want an attorney."

"You're not being charged with anything,

you moron," Farrell said. "We just need to con-
firm your alibi."

"We can find her, Mr. Reeves," I said. "We
know you were at the Casablanca last night.
Someone must have seen you together. It's only
time and effort."

"How do you know I was at the Casablanca?"

"You just said so."

"Smart bitch," Reeves said and leaned forward and hit me with his fist on my thigh. I've
had passes made at me that hurt more, but it
was all Farrell needed. He was on his feet, got
a handful of Reeves's hair, yanked him out of
the chair, and slammed him facedown on the
living room floor. He put his right knee
between Reeves's shoulder blades.

"We got you for assault, you sonofabitch."

Reeves started screaming. "Don't hurt me,
don't hurt me."

"You are under arrest for assault," Farrell
began. "You have the right to an attorney. If
you..."

"Bonnie Winslow," Reeves screamed.
"Bonnie Winslow was here."

Farrell grinned.

"If he gives us her address, are you willing
to drop the assault charge," he said to me.

"I guess," I said.

CHAPTER

16

LEE FARRELL CALLED to say that Lawrence B. Reeves's alibi checked out, and I was about fifteen minutes late meeting Julie at the bar in the Casablanca. When I got there, she was talking to a man with a blond beard wearing a dark brown Harris tweed jacket and a wool scarf. The wool scarf was not my favorite look. She had an empty wineglass in front of her and was just ordering another, when I slid onto the empty bar stool beside her.

"Sunny," she said, "this is Robert."

"Hi, Robert."

"Sunny?" Robert said. "What kind of name is Sunny?"

"A good one," I said.

The bartender delivered Julie's wine. I ordered a Belvedere martini on the rocks with a twist. Julie looked startled.

"Well," she said, "that kind of day."

"Yes."

Julie drank some of her white wine.

"I'm in the mood for wine myself," Robert said. "Maybe we should share a bottle."

"Sure," Julie said.

The bartender brought me my martini. I drank some and felt it move through me. I felt like saying *ahhhhh* but decided that it was unladylike.

"Want to talk about it?" Julie said.

"What kind of wine do you prefer?" Robert said.

"Oh, you pick it. I just know white and red," Julie said.

"I had to do something that makes me feel bad," I said.

"Did you have a choice?"

"Not really."

"Tell me," Julie said.

Robert was studying the wine list.

"How about this nice California Chardonnay," Robert said.

"Sure," Julie said.

Robert gestured to the bartender. I told Julie about Lawrence B. Reeves and Mary Lou Goddard, and Lee Farrell."

"Is the detective cute?" Julie said.

"And taken," I said.

"Aren't they all," Julie said. "You did what you had to do, Sunny."

The bartender brought a bottle of Chardonnay and two fresh glasses. He opened the wine and poured a small splash into one of the glasses.

"Would you care to test this?" Robert said to Julie.

"No, no. You decide," Julie said and smiled at him as if deciding were definitely man's work. She turned back to me.

"I know," I said, "but it doesn't make me feel good."

"Your client didn't have the right," Julie said, "to put you in that position."

I nodded. Robert sampled the wine as if he were testing the cure for cancer. He swirled the wine, breathed in its aroma, swirled it again, took a small sip, let it rest on his palate for a time before he swallowed, then nodded at the bartender, who poured out two glasses and left the bottle. Julie finished her existing wine and pushed the glass away and took the new wine. Robert leaned forward to talk to me across Julie.

"Would you care for some wine, Sunny?"

"No thanks," I said. "The martini is a nice year."

He smiled indulgently. Many members of the lower class didn't understand about wine. He clicked glasses with Julie and they each sipped some wine. Robert said something I couldn't hear, and Julie giggled. I thought about how odd Lawrence B. Reeves was. I thought about him here probably at this bar, with Bonnie Winslow. I thought it wouldn't do any harm to learn more about him, even if I wasn't on the case anymore. It was better than trying to talk to Julie, or listening to her talk with Robert, and really a whole hell of a lot better than listening to her giggle. I got one of my pictures of Lawrence out of my purse and showed it to the bartender.

"Larry Reeves," he said.

"He a regular?"

"Sure. Comes in couple nights a week."

"Alone?"

"When he comes in."

"He meet someone?"

"Usually picks up a woman," the bartender said. "That's what he comes in for. Nurses maybe one beer at the bar until he scores or strikes out."

"Does he score often?"

"Pretty often."

"He doesn't look like he would."

The bartender shrugged.

"Larry does pretty well, Sunny," he said. "This is Cambridge. Usual rules don't apply."

"Do you know any of the women he, ah, dates?"

"He scores a couple regulars pretty often," the bartender said.

"You know them?"

"Woman named Bonnie, some others, I don't know their names."

"Any of them here tonight?"

The bartender glanced around the bar. At this hour it was half empty.

He said, "Nope. Are you working, Sunny?"

"Not really," I said. "Just curious."

"If this is about a case or something, I probably shouldn't be blabbing."

"I don't even have a client," I said. "And I'll never tell you told."

"Sure," he said. "You want another martini?"

"I don't think so," I said.

Beside me, Julie and Robert had turned on their bar stools so that they were facing each other and their knees were sort of interactive. Julie giggled again. This wasn't a Julie I knew. And I wasn't sure it was a Julie I liked. There would be, however, a better time than now to discuss it. I thought about that for a while, and when my martini was gone, excused myself. Robert said it was great to meet me. Julie hugged me and said she hoped I felt better tomorrow. I said I was feeling better now. Julie said she'd call me. And I went home.

CHAPTER

17

I WAS SITTING at the bar of a restaurant in Wellesley called Blue Ginger with Spike.

"This is how it's going to go. Elizabeth has a blind date. She's afraid to meet him alone, so we'll sit here, and when she comes in she'll be thrilled to see us and ask us to join them."

"I haven't been this far out into the suburbs since the Brady Bunch was on television," Spike said.

"Elizabeth picked it. She thinks the city is dangerous."

Spike was drinking vodka on the rocks. He sipped some.

"I hate your sister," Spike said.

"I'm not crazy about her either, but she is family."

Spike said, "This is a big favor, Sunny."

"Yes it is, but I'm worth a big favor."

"Richie wouldn't do it?"

"I have dinner with Richie every Wednesday night," I said. "I wouldn't let her share that."

"So why not have dinner with her alone?"

"She's got a date, and she wants me to have one."

"Do I have to make out with you after?"

"No."

"Where'd she find this guy?"

I looked at the surface of my drink.

"Personal ad," I said very softly.

"What?"

"Personal ad," I said a little louder.

"Jesus Christ," Spike said.

"I know."

"Sunny, that's really embarrassing," Spike said.

"I know."

Spike drank off the rest of his vodka and pointed at the bartender for a refill.

"This is a really, really big favor," he said.

"I know."

"And there's a really, really unpleasant-looking guy sitting alone at a table for four," Spike said. "You know this guy's name?"

"No. Elizabeth didn't want us to meet him until she got here."

"Hope it's not him."

I looked at the man.

"Oh God," I said. "I hope not."

He was fiftyish, and overweight. He had on sunglasses and a bad toupee. He wore a dark double-breasted suit and a white dress shirt, with no tie. The collar of the shirt was folded out over the lapels of his jacket, and the top three buttons were open. He wore some sort of necklace but I was too far away to see clearly, and while I feared he'd be showing a lot of gray chest hair, I was too far away to see that either. He had a drink in front of him, and now and then he looked at his watch.

Spike said, "Oh, Jesus," and nodded toward the door.

"Elizabeth," I said.

She was wearing sunglasses too. Her hair was freshly done. She had on three-inch sling-back heels, and a mink coat, which she wore open over a tiny black dress that was just long enough to conceal her lingerie—if any.

"If these two are in fact together," Spike said, "somebody's going to call the cops."

"Pray with me," I said.

Elizabeth spoke to the hostess, who led her to the table where the hideous man was seated. He rose when she arrived. She gave him her hand. He kissed it.

"We're fucked," Spike said.

Elizabeth smiled brightly and turned toward us at the bar and gestured for us to join them. Spike gulped his second vodka. I got off the bar stool and smiled at Elizabeth. While I was smiling, I murmured under my breath to Spike.

"We certainly are," I said.

We walked over and joined them. The man's name was Mort Kraken. He did in fact have gray chest hair, and the necklace was a thick gold chain with a large medallion on the end. I didn't look closely enough to see what kind of a medallion it was.

"So you two married?" he said.

"No."

"I been married," Mort said. "But then I found out you could get the milk for free, and you didn't have to buy the cow."

Spike leaned back a little in his chair and glanced up at the ceiling.

"Good thinking," I said desperately.

I put my hand on Spike's thigh. If Spike started on him, it would be the worst evening of Mort's life. The waitress approached.

"So who's drinking what?" Mort said. "First round's on me."

Did this mean that at the end of the evening we'd be puzzling out the check as to who had paid for what round and which of us had ordered a salad? The thought of Spike's reaction to that was chilling. I ordered a martini. Spike ordered Gray Goose on the rocks.

Mort said, "Me and the lady will have a couple Champagne cocktails."

Elizabeth smiled. She had allowed her mink coat to fall over the back of her chair revealing that the little black dress was held up by two very thin spaghetti straps, maybe vermicelli straps, and covered her top half about as well as the skirt covered her bottom, which was to say barely.

"That's all I drink," Mort said with a firm leveling gesture. He had a big pinkie ring. "Nothing else. Always Champagne cocktails."

I still had my hand on Spike's thigh. I could feel him quiver slightly.

"So tell me, Mort, what do you do for work?" Elizabeth said brightly.

She was leaning toward him, her lips parted slightly. She was wearing a lot of eye makeup and her heavy eyelids seemed almost to be fluttering. I thought I might retch.

"I'm rich," he said, and leaned back in his chair and laughed very loudly. "That's what I do for work, pretty lady, I'm rich."

"How'd you get rich?" Spike said.

My breath came a little easier. He was trying to be civil.

"Hey, he talks," Mort said.

Good Jesus! I squeezed Spike's thigh. I could hear Spike breathe in.

"Not often," Spike said. "How'd you get rich?"

Mort made a *mezzo-mezzo* gesture with his other hand. Another pinkie ring. Every revelation was appalling. I smiled at him warmly.

"Little of this, little of that," Mort said. "It's just some kind of genetic thing, you know. Everything I do I make money."

"That's really nice," Elizabeth said.

She was entirely taken with him; she gazed at him as if there were no one else in the room. I knew Elizabeth was far more snobby than I, and, therefore, experienced Mort to be considerably less than a cockroach. I had to admire her commitment to dating. The drinks arrived. Spike consumed half of his, and I noticed that Elizabeth inhaled a lot of her Champagne cocktail in one snort. Mort raised his glass.

"Good times," he said. "Where'd you get the name Spike?"

"My mother's maiden name," Spike said.

"You mean it's your real name."

"Um hm."

"Goddamn. My real name's Mortimer. Lotta people think Mort is short for Morton, but it's not. It's short for Mortimer."

"Really," I said.

The waitress distributed the menus. Mort didn't even look at his.

"Talk to them," he said, nodding at Spike and me. "Me and the pretty lady are going to have Chateaubriand for two with all the trimmings."

"I'm sorry," the waitress said. "We really don't have anything like that."

"What the hell kind of joint did you drag me to," Mort said to Elizabeth, then to the waitress, "How about Beef Wellington."

"This is really Pacific Rim cuisine," the waitress said. "I can ask in the kitchen if they could make some sort of beef dish for you."

Elizabeth would not look at me.

"Naw, we'll have whatever they're having," Mort said.

He leaned back in his chair and draped one arm around the back of Elizabeth's chair, and looked pleased with himself for having put one over on the waitress. We ordered.

"So," Mort said to me. "Did you two say you were married?"

"Oh, no," Elizabeth said, "they're just friends."

"Sure," Mort said and gave me a slow wink. "I've heard that story before."

"I'm gay," Spike said.

"Excuse me?"

"I'm gay."

Mort looked a little flustered for a moment as if something had actually penetrated the chain mail of his stupidity.

"I didn't know. I mean, Christ, you don't look gay."

Spike smiled. It was not a pleasant smile, but I don't think Mort knew that.

"My shorts are lavender," Spike said.

"Spike," I said. "Do you love me?"

"Yes."

"I knew you did," I said.

Spike looked at me, and at Mort, and took a long deep breath. He nodded slowly to himself and let the breath out slowly through his nose and smiled slowly at me, and picked up his glass and took a long slow swallow of vodka. He looked thoughtfully at Elizabeth and Mort.

"I hope they don't breed," he said.

CHAPTER

18

I FOUND BONNIE Winslow in the phone book and went to her home and showed her my license. She invited me to have some tea with her and her three cats, on the second floor of two-family house with white aluminum siding, in Watertown.

"Tell me a little about Lawrence Reeves," I said.

Bonnie was short and sharp-featured with long blond-streaked gray hair. She had on jeans and sandals and a big orange tee shirt not tucked in, on which was printed LOVE IS CONTAGIOUS.

"Why do you ask?" Bonnie said.

"Background check," I said.

"And who might your client be?" she said.

No fool, Bonnie. I smiled ruefully.

"I'm sorry, Bonnie. May I call you Bonnie?"

"Of course."

"I'm sorry, Bonnie, but the background check has to remain confidential."

"May I see your credentials again," Bonnie said.

"Certainly."

Bonnie looked at my license for a while but it didn't tell her anything it hadn't told her the first time.

"Is there a problem talking about Mr. Reeves?" I said. "I can simply put you down as 'declined to comment,' if you wish."

"No, no, of course not," Bonnie said. "I'm just not a person who starts gossiping about a friend the minute someone asks."

"I can see that," I said.

"What would you like to know."

"I need to just establish your relationship for the record," I said. "Is he your boyfriend?"

"Oh, Larry and I are just old friends."

"You spent the night with him last Tuesday," I said.

"Who told you that?"

"Is that a part of the friendship?"

Bonnie smiled.

"Larry and I are both consenting adults. Occasionally when each of us is without a partner, we share an evening like that."

"I gather he has other partners."

"Oh Larry plays the field all right." Bonnie smiled again. "I guess, if the truth be told, so do I."

"Isn't that a little risky?" I said.

"You mean infection? We're very careful."

"Do you know any of Larry's other partners?"

"Some."

"Do you know Mary Lou Goddard?"

"Oh, that snoot."

"Snoot?"

"Yes, Larry told me about her. He went out with her a couple of times and then she got possessive."

"Possessive?"

"You know, he could only go out with her. He couldn't see me anymore or any of his other friends."

"How did Larry feel about that?" I said.

"Larry likes to play the field."

"Was he angry with her?"

"Larry? Don't be silly. Larry has lots of girls."

"Was she angry with him?"

"I guess so. Larry told me that he blew her off. Told her he had other fish to fry and that he didn't have time for small-minded, narrow people like her."

"Larry likes to keep his options open," I said without expression.

"Exactly."

I had mastered her lingo.

"You know any of his other friends?"

"Female friends? Not really. There was one named Charlene something, and a girl named Sophie. He often met new friends at the bar."

"Casablanca?"

"Sometimes, any of the bars around Harvard Square."

"Has Larry ever been married?" I said.

"Oh yes. I think that's why he's so footloose and fancy-free now," Bonnie said. "I guess little Harriet gave him a pretty hard time."

"You know her?"

"I feel like I do, Larry talks about her so much, but I don't. She must have been awful."

"They're divorced."

"I guess."

"She keep her married name?"

"Yes. It drove Larry crazy."

"Where does she live?" I said.

"I don't know, around here somewhere, Larry mentions running into her now and then. He hates that."

I finished my tea. The cats ignored me. They probably smelled Rosie on me and didn't like it. About which I was pleased. Bonnie told me a few stories about her love life, which made me think I might have to reconsider mine. And spoke so glowingly about Larry that I wanted to ask for his card. If I couldn't use it, I could pass it on to my sister.

CHAPTER

19

IT WAS JULIE'S turn to come to me, so we met for lunch in the dining room of the Boston Harbor Hotel. Julie was having some white wine while she heard about my dinner with Elizabeth. I had some cranberry juice with club soda and a slice of orange.

"Elizabeth thinks people are beneath contempt if they went to a state university. Why would she date Mort, who is hideous beyond the power of language?"

"How about beauty is in the eye of the beholder?" Julie said.

"Anyone who beheld him would find him hideous," I said. "I was in mortal fear that Spike was going to reach over and twist his head off."

"Maybe his failures are his charm," Julie said. She drank some wine.

"Oh boy, is that a shrinky remark," I said, "or what?"

"Maybe he embodies her condition. Maybe she feels so lousy about herself that he's what she can relate to."

The waitress came and took our order.

Julie had a second glass of wine. It was late for lunch, nearly two. We had a table by the window in the half-empty dining room. Beyond the glass the harbor looked so energetically blue-collar. The boats moved about briskly bouncing on the chop kicked up by an onshore wind. The pilings of some of the piers were rotting and the water near them was iridescent with oil slick. An occasional piece of buoyant litter moved in the tidal eddies around the pilings.

"You didn't used to drink at lunch," I said.

"Well now I do."

I nodded and sipped my cranberry spritzer.

"You have a problem with that?" Julie said.

"Do you?"

"If I do," Julie said, "I'll let you know."

"Sure," I said. "You seen Robert since the other night?"

"Oh Robert's nothing. He's just fun."

I nodded again and sipped my cranberry spritzer some more. One of the big, slick-looking, mostly glass Boston Harbor tour boats slid out past us, leaving a big smooth wake. A couple of seagulls bobbed on the wake.

"Did you go home with him the other night?"

Julie stared at me. She turned her wineglass by the stem slowly.

"At least you didn't start with *It's none of my business but…,*" Julie said. "I hate when people do that."

"Me too," I said.

She turned her wineglass some more. The waitress brought us our salads and departed.

"Don't ask me things like that," Julie said.

I nodded.

"I'll take that as a yes," I said.

"Take it any way you wish."

"I wish for your happiness, Jule. You've been the sister I never had for nearly all our lives."

Julie reached across the table and patted my hand.

"I know, Sunny. I know."

"And being a trained detective," I said, "I have observed signs that you are not happy."

"Well good for you, Nancy Drew."

"Is it Michael?"

"Would you accept *none of your business?*"

"No."

"I didn't think you would," Julie said. "How about, *I don't want to talk about it?*"

"No."

Julie drank the rest of her wine and looked around for the waitress. We were quiet while the waitress resupplied her. Our salads remained before us, unmolested.

"I love Michael," Julie said.

I nodded.

"But we probably got married too soon."

I nodded.

"I never had a life of my own. I moved from my father's house to my husband's house."

"And?"

"And we had the kids and I have never made an adult decision based solely on what was best for me."

"And you've decided it's time," I said.

"Yes."

"And your first two decisions are to drink more than you used to and sleep with a guy you met at a bar."

"God, Sunny, don't lecture me."

"I'm merely observing. Am I right or wrong?"

"Well, if you insist on putting it that way..."

Julie's face had reddened a little.

"Put it any way you'd like," I said. "I'm only trying to track your decisions."

"Goddamit, it's a start," Julie said.

"What's your next step," I said.

"You make this sound like some kind of fucking marketing strategy, Sunny. I don't know my next step. I'm trying to breathe. I'm trying to get some space around myself so I can see who I am."

"I understand," I said, "I sympathize. I'm on your side. But maybe the way you're doing things isn't the best way."

"What the fuck do you know about it," Julie said.

Her eyes were starting to tear.

"Been there," I said softly, "done that."

Julie started to cry though it was a restrained crying. Not a lot of loud boo-hoo. Just a little trouble with her breathing and some tears on her cheeks.

"Oh God, Sunny, of course you have. I'm sorry."

"You do it the way you have to," I said. "If I can help, I will. Just remember that right now, you're crazy, so don't make irrevocable decisions. If you feel like you want to, call a wise and stable private detective and discuss it with her."

She nodded her head. I put my hand out across the table. She took it and held on.

"And you might see a shrink," I said.

She nodded again and smiled a little.

"In addition to you?" Julie said, trying to steady her voice.

"I'm not actually licensed," I said, "in that area."

CHAPTER

20

Rosie and I had run along Summer Street. Rosie had breakfasted, and I was on my second cup of coffee, when Lee Farrell called me.

"Thought you'd want to know. Lawrence B. Reeves killed himself last night."

"How?"

"Sat on his couch in his living room, put a .357 mag in his mouth, and pulled the trigger," Farrell said.

"He didn't seem the type," I said. "No question on the suicide?"

"Who is the type?" Farrell said.

"I don't mean to kill himself. I mean to use a .357."

"No reason to doubt it. Powder residue on his hand and face. Track of the bullet consistent with a self-inflicted wound. And there was a note."

"Really?"

"Says he hired somebody to kill Mary Lou. Didn't say who. Says the guy made a mistake, and Lawrence B. couldn't live with the guilt."

"Handwritten note?"

"Composed on a word processor, signed. The signature is authentic."

"He doesn't name the button man?" I said.

"Nope. Note says Lawrence B. takes full responsibility."

Rosie went to her water dish and began to lap noisily. It was never clear to me how a thirty-one-pound dog could drink fifty pounds of water, but there was much I didn't understand, and I was calm about it.

"Two birds with the same stone," I said. "Clears up a homicide for Cambridge and a homicide in Boston."

"Yes it do," Farrell said. "Except for who Lawrence hired, and you know how good our chances there are."

"I don't like it," I said.

"I'm sorry."

"You don't like it either," I said, "which is why you're calling me up."

"I'm a courteous guy," Farrell said.

"A guy like Lawrence B. Reeves," I said, "would not know where to hire a shooter. And he would not know which end of a .357 magnum to put in his mouth. Moreover, if he was contrite enough to kill himself, why wouldn't he name the shooter?"

"No case is perfect," Farrell said.

"Did you match the bullet that killed Reeves with the ones that killed Gretchen Crane?

"Crane was killed with a .22."

"Then trying to match them doesn't make much sense."

"You really know your ordnance," Farrell said.

"It's a gift," I said. "It's probably hard to convince anyone to pursue the investigation when this conclusion explains two of them so neatly."

"Sunny, that's cynical," Farrell said.

"I was afraid it might sound that way," I said.

"There's a key on a nail on the right-hand side of the porch, under the overhang. Don't you dare touch it."

"I'll try not to," I said. "But you know about nosy broads."

"I do," Farrell said.

I hung up, and went down to my easel, under the skylight. The sun slanted in from the east just right at this time of day and I always tried to take advantage of it. From long experience Rosie knew what would happen and trotted down to the easel ahead of me and sat in the warm rhomboid of sunlight that splashed across the floor. I was working on a painting of the former city hall from a perspective on Tremont, across the Kings Chapel Burial Grounds. And I was having trouble with the gray. Painting always completely absorbed the parts of my brain required to do it, and consequently untethered the other parts and let them meander where they would. Today they meandered over the array of sexual conundrums I had in my case load. I had no idea what to do about my sister Elizabeth. I hadn't spoken with her since we dined with the loathsome Mort. Maybe I wasn't supposed to do anything about her. Maybe she was a consenting adult. I had even less idea what to do about Julie. She too was a consenting adult. Maybe I wasn't supposed to do anything about her either. I wondered how much part her husband and children were having in her consent. Someone, maybe Larry himself, had taken care of what to do about Lawrence B. Reeves, who liked to smack bitches. And what was up with Mary Lou Goddard, who was as militant a lesbian as I could remember meeting, and appeared to have been engaged in heterosexuality with the late Larry? There was enough wrong with the suicide to invite further investigation. And since I knew how to investigate, it was that path that beckoned.

Sunny, I said, you don't have a client on this case.

I know, I said, but I don't have any other clients on any other cases, either. And I can't paint twelve hours a day.

Farrell's right, I said. I am a nosy girl.

I believe *you* said that; Farrell just agreed.

Whatever.

I mixed a little blue into the gray on my palette, and tried it out. Rosie sat in her sun patch and watched me with her tongue hanging out. Now and then she took a break and inspected the white tip on her tail for a while. I painted until the sun moved away and then I put my paints away, cleaned up, and thought about detecting.

CHAPTER

21

IT WAS SHARED-custody time. I dropped Rosie off with Richie at work. She knew where she was going as soon as I pulled up in front of the saloon on Portland Street. I had trouble holding her still while I snapped on her leash, and she pulled me at an undignified speed across the sidewalk and into the bar. Richie was leaning on the end of the bar talking to one of the bartenders, while two or three early customers were getting their hearts going along the bar. I felt what I always felt when I saw him: love, a little fear, some desire, and some thrills I can't define. I unsnapped Rosie's leash and she flew at Richie and spun around several times in the process. He squatted on his haunches and let her lap his face for a bit.

"Hi," I said.

He picked Rosie up and stood and held her while she lapped his neck and wagged her tail very fast.

"Richie, there are people who won't believe this when I tell them," the bartender said.

"There are people who might be tending bar at the no-tell motel in West Boylston, Jim," Richie said.

Jim grinned.

"Mum's the word," he said.

Richie smiled at me.

"You want to lap my face too?"

"Maybe if I just raced across the floor and did a couple of spins," I said.

He leaned forward and I kissed him lightly on the lips. Richie put Rosie down and she went around behind the bar to say hello to Jim.

"I usually give her a little piece of pickled kielbasa," Jim said. "That okay?"

"Sure," Richie said.

"Not too much though," I said. "I don't want her to turn into a porklet."

"See why we got divorced," Richie said.

"She's had breakfast," I said, "and a walk and pooped and peeped and done everything she's supposed to."

"Good girl," Richie said.

Richie's father and his uncles ran the Irish mob in Massachusetts. Richie had to my knowledge never been a part of it, except to run the legitimate things they owned, like the saloon. We used to argue about it. I said the money was dirty. Richie said maybe, but he hadn't earned it in a dirty way, and family was family. We had never resolved the argument, probably because both of us were right.

Richie was dark Irish. His hair was black and thick and short. He had to shave twice a day if he was going out at night. He wasn't big exactly, but he seemed big, and there was about him a contained strength that made him seem dangerous. Which he could be. Though never to me, or Rosie. I thought he was about as handsome a man as I had ever met.

"We're still on for dinner tomorrow night," I said.

"Yes."

"Good. I'll pick her up then."

Jim had found a ball from Rosie's last visit and was rolling it across the barroom floor. Rosie was racing after it, skidding a little on the polished floor and rushing it back so he'd throw it again. One of the morning boozers at the bar said, "Man, I don't need that with a hangover."

Nobody paid any attention to him. He looked annoyed. He spoke to Richie.

"The mutt gotta do that?"

Richie turned his head slowly and looked at the man. He didn't say anything. The man looked uncomfortable. Richie kept looking at him. The man stopped looking at Richie and went back to his CC and ginger. Rosie dashed across the floor again and grabbed the ball and hustled it back behind the bar. She had to wait a moment while Jim poured another drink for the complaining barfly.

"You working on anything?" Richie said.

"I'm sort of involved in that woman that was murdered downtown."

"The feminist?"

"Worked for a feminist consulting company," I said. "The police think it might have been a contract hit."

"Really?"

"You haven't heard anything, have you?"

"A lot of murders go down in this city without me being consulted," Richie said.

"I know. I just wondered."

"I hear anything I'll tell you."

"Thanks," I said. "I gotta go. You'll be sure to walk her."

"I'll be sure," Richie said.

I went around the bar and patted Rose good-bye and came back and gave Richie a light kiss.

"Sunny?"

"Yes."

"You look really good," he said.

"You do too, Richie."

We both stood.

"I'll see you tomorrow night," I said.

"Yes."

I put my arms around him and hugged him hard. I could feel the muscles in his back, and I remembered how strong he was. He hugged me back. We let go slowly.

"Bye," I said.

"Bye."

CHAPTER

22

MOST PEOPLE HAVE a spare key hanging around somewhere, and a patient burglar could make a pretty easy living looking in mailboxes and under doormats. Lawrence B. Reeves had been a little more inventive. If Farrell hadn't told me where it was, it would have taken at least five minutes for me to find it hanging on a small nail concealed on the right side of the porch where the decking overhung a couple of inches.

I went in. The place already had the stale smell of a place that has been closed for a while without occupancy. Though my memory was that it hadn't smelled that good the last time I was here. I was in the living room where Lawrence had, so to speak, volunteered the name of Bonnie Winslow. There was a dark bloodstain still on the back of the couch. Sections of *The Boston Globe,* datelined the day he killed himself, were scattered on the floor by the couch. Two cans of beer sat on the coffee table in front of the couch. I picked them up. One was empty, one was half empty.

People often got drunk to kill themselves, I knew. But a beer and a half? Of course, given the state of Lawrence's housekeeping maybe the two cans had been there for a week.

I moved through the house. There were unwashed dishes piled in the sink, and a white plastic drawstring trash bag that was beginning to reek of garbage. The bed was unmade. The bathroom fixtures were unscrubbed. There was mildew in the shower stall. In the den there was an antique mahogany desk with three drawers, and a leatherette Barcalounger. You don't see a lot of Barcaloungers anymore. In point of fact you don't see a lot of leatherette anymore.

I stood in the den and let what I'd seen on my first sweep coalesce. There seemed to be nothing untoward, merely the suspended animation of a life interrupted. The place needed to be mucked out and ventilated and scrubbed. I wondered if there were next of kin. I felt like cleaning the place myself but was afraid it would reveal a deep-rooted housewifely-ness.

I took a big breath and started the second sweep, the one I really didn't like, which involved opening drawers and rummaging through dirty laundry.

Looking in his desk I learned that he drew a paycheck from Boston University, though from the size of it, it was probably part-time. His checkbook had a balance of less than a hundred dollars. He was delinquent in most of his bills. He had a considerable balance outstanding on his Visa card, where he apparently paid the minimum each month. Going through his check stubs revealed that there was no sign of a significant check for cash, nor a check, however implausible, that could have been used to pay a hit man. On his most recent credit card bill there were three charges to a flower shop in Harvard Square. There was no sign of flowers in the apartment. I made a note. There was also a one-night charge for a room at a motel in Natick. I made a note.

In the second drawer of the desk was a collection of atrocious erotic poetry written in lavender ink on blue-lined paper in what looked to my innocent eye to be a woman's hand. I forced myself the read them. They were clearly addressed to Lawrence B., who was apparently a better lovemaker than I would have given him credit for. Unless, of course, the poet was taking artistic liberties. If she was, it was as close to artistic as she got. When I got through with the poetry, things got much worse. I found several Polaroid snapshots of Bonnie Winslow in naked abandon, on what seemed to be Lawrence B.'s bed. I put them quickly away. It could have been worse; they could have been of Lawrence himself. I looked at his calendar. There were various meaningless notations including the letter *J* every Thursday.

I found his address book and glanced through it. Mary Lou's phone number and address were there. I put it and the calendar pad aside to take with me and consider at my leisure, if I ever got any leisure. I continued to rummage, and by the time I got through rummaging it was dark and the most significant thing I'd uncovered was something I hadn't found.

In my car I called Farrell.

"Nice to see you're still working," I said.

"We never sleep," Farrell said.

"Is there a .357 registered to Lawrence B. Reeves?" I said.

"No."

"But you assume the one he shot himself with was his."

"Lot of unregistered guns out there, Sunny."

"I know."

"Did you search Reeves's apartment?"

"Not in my jurisdiction," Farrell said. "Cambridge people maybe snooped a little."

"They find any ammunition?"

"Just the five rounds left in the piece."

"If you go out and buy a gun, don't you buy ammo?"

"Depends on where you get it."

"Okay, so you buy an illegal piece. Do you generally buy six rounds for it?"

"No, generally you buy a box of shells."

"There was no box of shells," I said. "I looked."

"What are you saying?"

"Have you traced the gun?"

"It's Cambridge's case. Just happens to close mine for me too."

"Maybe it would pay off," I said.

"I'm a city cop, Sunny. Like your old man. Like you were for a while. How many of us are dying to take an easy case and make it hard?"

"In round figures," I said, "about none."

"In that area," Farrell said. "However, if I can do anything easy to help you, call me."

"How about something hard?"

"Call Cambridge," Farrell said. "It's their case."

CHAPTER

23

Elizabeth said, "Well? What do you think?"

"Of Mort?"

"Yes."

Elizabeth had decided to get in shape for the single life, and to that end had begun to come in to Boston on a regular basis to work out with me. Since Elizabeth was not in top shape, to accommodate her I'd had to slow the workouts way down. My sister was, thus, simultaneously accomplishing two things: She was improving her physical condition and degrading mine.

"Whatever works," I said. "Do you enjoy him?"

"Enjoy him?"

We were walking, and not very briskly, along Summer Street. Rosie was straining on her leash as we picked our way through the traffic and construction. Elizabeth had on brand-new pink sweats with a little black designer trademark on the right hip of the sweatpants, and some pink walking shoes with pink-and-white candy-striped laces in them.

"Yes."

"Well, aren't you funny," Elizabeth said. "I never really ever thought about do I enjoy him."

"So how do you decide if you like him?" I said.

"He's an available man and he has money," Elizabeth said firmly.

"These are good qualities," I said.

We paused at a light near the Fargo Building. Two big trucks piled with excavated gravel lumbered past. The light turned. We crossed with Rosie leading out in full tug.

"She should be taught to heel," Elizabeth said. "I wouldn't have a dog that wasn't properly trained to the leash."

"Rosie could heel if she wanted to," I said.

"We're going on a cruise," Elizabeth said.

"On a boat?" I said.

"Of course on a boat. What did you think?"

"I thought you might be going to dress up like a Las Vegas lounge act, and go from bar to bar."

"What?"

"Just a little joke," I said.

"Mort's paying for everything."

"What a guy."

"What does that mean?"

"It means isn't that swell," I said.

"We're intimate of course."

"Of course," I said.

"Why 'of course'?"

Rosie discovered the empty wrapper to a Mounds bar crumpled in the corner of a building, and we came to a halt while she sniffed it very carefully.

"Most grown-ups when they are dating, become intimate," I said.

"Including you?"

"Including me," I said.

"Do you have much experience?"

"Not enough."

"Why 'not enough'?"

"Another weak gesture toward wit," I said. "Why do you ask?"

"Well..."

Elizabeth paused and watched Rosie sniff the candy wrapper, as if she found it interesting. I waited. Rosie concluded that there was nothing palatable left in the wrapper, and turned from it and leaned against the leash, ready to forge on. Elizabeth and I followed her. Elizabeth tried again.

"Do...?"

"Do what," I said.

"This is very difficult, Sunny. I never had sex with anyone but Hal."

"And now you have, and probably a good thing," I said.

I could almost hear Elizabeth inhale.

"Do all the men you go out with perform?"

"Oh," I said. "That's it."

"Well, do they?"

"Mostly," I said. "I don't think there are many women who haven't been with a man who drank too much, and wasn't, ah, up to the task. But it hasn't happened often."

"What do you do when that happens?"

"I assure him that it's okay, and kiss him

affectionately good night and thank him for the evening, and go home."

"Do you see him again?"

"It only happened to me once, that I remember," I said. "And no, I didn't see him again."

"Because he couldn't perform?"

"No. If I liked him, I could wait for another try. But if you get so drunk while you're with me that you can't, for lack of a better phrase, complete the evening, what does that say about where I stand?"

"Where you stand?"

A man with an Akita on a thick leash came along the sidewalk toward us. Rosie spotted him and stopped and got very low, her ears flat, her tail down. Given the size of the Akita I felt like doing the same thing. The man smiled and tightened the leash up so that he held the Akita against his leg and we passed each other with plenty of room.

When the crisis had passed and Rosie was back up and sprightly again, I said, "Yes. I insist on ranking above booze."

"I don't think Mort was drunk," she said.

"But he couldn't get it up."

"No. Is it my fault?"

"No."

"How can you be so sure?"

"Because you look like me," I said.

"No, seriously," Elizabeth said.

"I was serious."

"Well, besides that?"

"If you don't excite a man, he won't attempt your virtue in the first place," I said.

"Attempt my virtue?"

"He won't make a pass at you, Elizabeth. If Mort had taken you home and given you a peck on the cheek and said he'd call, then you might assume you didn't excite him. But if he attempted to have sex and failed, it's not you."

"I was afraid that when he saw me with my clothes off that he... I'm thirty-eight years old."

"It's not about you, Elizabeth. It's about him. Blood pressure medication. Stress. Maybe making all that money exhausts him."

"I tried my best," Elizabeth said. "I only know what worked with Hal, but I did everything I knew."

"How'd he feel about it?" I said.

"Him?"

"Yes."

"I don't know."

"Jesus Christ!"

I tried to keep the irritation out of my voice. I felt sort of bad for her. It was like talking to a self-absorbed child.

"Maybe you should move on," I said.

"To whom?"

"To the next guy that seems suitable. No rush. I like men, but I find it perfectly nice to be without one as needed. I'm enough."

"That's feminist propaganda. A woman without a man is nowhere, and you know it.

"Actually, hon, I don't know that."

"Men are where the bucks are," she said. "And anyone who pretends differently is just lying to themselves."

"So you're going to keep seeing Mort?"

"Absolutely."

"And when the evening's over you'll go home and, what, grope him?"

"It's where the bucks are," she said. "You'd do exactly the same thing."

If I was quick, I could push her in front of one of the fill trucks moving along Summer Street. She would be out of her misery. I would be out of mine. I could plead justifiable homicide.

"You would," Elizabeth said. "You know you would."

"Sure," I said. "Sure I would."

CHAPTER

24

I WAS IN a store in Cambridge called the Blossom Shop, talking to the owner, a black-haired woman with a short haircut, in black jeans and a black turtleneck, wearing gold-framed granny glasses. She had pale skin, a lot of dark eye makeup, and black lipstick.

"Your name wouldn't be Addams, would it?" I said.

She told me her name was Blossom.

"Like the shop," she said.

"Isn't that adorable," I said. "I'm working with Detective Larkin."

"I don't know any cops."

I handed her a Xerox of the credit card statement.

"There are three charges for flowers," I said. "I need to know who received them."

"You say you're with the police?"

"Sure."

"Let me check."

She went to the back of the store and sat down at a computer and fiddled with it for a bit.

"All three orders went to Mary Lou Goddard, in Chestnut Hill. You want the address?"

"No. I know it."

"Is this an important clue?" Blossom said.

"It might be," I said. "Watch the newspapers."

After I left Blossom, I got my car and went up to Central Square to talk with Larkin. I found a parking space outside the police station on the curb by a sign that said police vehicles only. Larkin was in the squad room on the second floor, with five other detectives. He stood when I approached his desk, snagged a straight chair from next to another desk, and put it beside his. I sat down.

"Farrell called me. You've been doing some illegal entry."

"Exactly," I said.

There was a picture of a woman and three small children framed on Larkin's desk.

"You're not satisfied that Reeves killed himself?"

"No."

"We like the theory," Larkin said.

"Farrell likes it too. Did you happen to trace the gun?"

Larkin shrugged. He had blond hair combed straight back, a thin reddish face, and a thick red-blond moustache. He wore a gold wedding band on his left hand.

"Not so far," he said. "Nobody here figures it's a high priority."

"It's not registered to Reeves?"

"Sunny, when you were a cop, how were the gun records?"

"Chaos."

Larkin smiled.

"So," I said, "we don't even know if it's Reeves's gun."

"Could have bought it out of state," Larkin said. "Could have bought it illegally. Could have bought it down the street, filled out all the forms, and some clerk in Boston filed it under Zbigniew."

"Anybody issue him a permit?"

"We haven't."

"But somebody might have."

"Yep."

"It's something that could be ascertained."

" 'Ascertained'? Wow, Sunny. You're some talker."

"But it could be," I said.

"Sure. Eventually."

"Could you look into that?"

Larkin grinned at me.

"You ever think how blond our kids would be if we mated?" he said.

"All the time," I said. "See what you can find out for me about the gun."

"Will it improve our chances of mating?"

"Won't hurt them," I said. I nodded at the picture on his desk. "They might."

Larkin looked at the picture and smiled.

"Yeah," he said. "They always do."

I went across the river and got on the Mass Pike and drove out to Natick. The motel I was after was done up like a Norman castle. But I wasn't fooled. I parked in the lot and went into the lobby and asked at the desk for the manager. The manager wasn't available but the assistant manager was in. He would do.

The assistant manager's name was Mr. Francis. His office was small and neat. He was tall, slim, and neat. Gray suit, red tie, white shirt, new haircut, a hint of cologne.

"My name is Randall," I said. "I'm working with the Boston Police Department on a murder suicide, and I need a little information."

I sort of mumbled the "working with" part, but he was too slick for me.

"I hate to trouble you," he said, "but may I see some identification?"

I handed some over. He read it.

"You're a private detective," he said.

"Yes."

It didn't seem to trouble him. He was employed to please people.

"How can I help?"

"I have a listing on a credit card bill, for a night at this hotel. I wonder if you could tell me who stayed here?"

"I can tell you who registered here, which may not, of course, be the same thing."

"I know," I said. "I'd be grateful for anything you can tell me."

He took the bill and smiled and excused himself and left the office. In about five minutes he was back. His files were obviously in better shape than those in the state gun office.

"Mr. and Mrs. Lawrence B. Reeves," he said. "From Cambridge."

"Do you suppose anyone would remember Mrs. Reeves?"

"Almost certainly not," Mr. Francis said. "It was more than a month ago. We check people in and out one hundred a day or more. Unless there was something unusual..."

"Perhaps if I could talk with the clerk," I said.

"I'd have to check the personnel records to see who was on duty, which would take some time and effort, and believe me, no one is going to remember a face unless there was some reason to. Is there anything unusual about these people?"

"Not in the sense you mean," I said.

"Then it would waste everybody's time. If you work with the public you tend to blur them in self-defense."

He was right, and I knew it. So I thanked him and left. Was it Mary Lou he'd shacked up with? It might have been. It was obviously covert, otherwise why drive out to Natick and check into a hotel? Why not take her to his love nest in Cambridge the way he had Bonnie? This was someone who didn't want to be known. Somebody whose professional credentials included being a feminist lesbian. I thought I might have a clue. How exciting. Buoyed by success, I drove back into Boston to talk with someone at Boston University.

Since I was slouching toward a distant M.F.A. at B. U., I knew where to park and where to ask. But for all I learned there about Lawrence B. Reeves, I could have been a student in hydraulic repair at Wentworth. Lawrence B. was a part-time instructor in philosophy in the night school and had been for the last five years. He had a master's degree in philosophy from the University of Wisconsin, and, according to the résumé in his personnel file, had completed the course work for a Ph.D. and was listed as ABD (all but dissertation). Like a lot of people teaching nights in large urban schools, Lawrence didn't seem to be a finisher.

CHAPTER

25

IN THE MORNING, showered, with my hair nearly perfect, full of good coffee and an oatmeal scone with maple frosting, I went downtown to talk with Mary Lou Goddard at her office. The bloodstained rug in the outer office had been replaced. Mary Lou was in her office, separated from the lower orders by glass partitioning. She looked at me with restrained distaste when I was shown in by her secretary.

"I want nothing to do with you, Ms. Randall."

"I know why," I said.

"I made it very clear to you why, when I discharged you."

"I know about you and Lawrence Reeves. I know about you and him at Locksley Hall Hotel in Natick."

I knew no such thing. I had no evidence that his guest that night was Mary Lou. It was a guess. And it was a good one. Mary Lou looked as if I had offered to eviscerate her. She sat and stared at me for a moment, then got up and crossed the room and closed the door and went back and sat behind her desk again.

"What do you want?" she said after a while.

"I want to know the truth," I said.

Actually my hopes were more modest than that, but it implied that I knew more than I actually did, and it had a nice dramatic ring to it. Maybe she'd snarl, *You can't handle the truth*. But maybe she'd say something that would tell me something useful.

"Who else knows about this?" Mary Lou said softly.

"I haven't told anyone," I said. "I don't know what Farrell and Larkin know."

"Who are they?"

"Farrell's the Boston detective you talked with," I said. "Larkin is a Cambridge detective. Reeves died in Cambridge."

"Why won't you leave this alone," Mary Lou said.

Her voice seemed more sad than angry. It wasn't a bad question. I was quiet while I thought about it.

"I'm a detective," I said. "That means, concretely, that I like to detect things; and, abstractly, that I have some concern with justice."

"What kind of an answer is that?" Mary Lou said. "That answer makes no sense to me."

"I'll rephrase it," I said. "I won't leave *this* alone, because *this*, whatever it quite is, is what I do."

"Freud said that love and work are what matter most to people."

"Um hm."

"And this is your work."

"Um hm."

"Even though no one is paying you."

"No one is paying me either way," I said. "I'm between cases."

"But not out of work," Mary Lou said.

"Exactly," I said. "So why didn't you tell me about Lawrence B. Reeves?"

Mary Lou put her fingertips carefully together in front of her chest and leaned back in her spring chair and examined the pyramid her hands made.

"The name of this organization is Great Strides," she said. "We consult on women's issues from a feminist perspective. I am an avowed and public lesbian, which tends to underscore our perspective."

"And a fling with a man would be bad for business," I said.

"Bad for everything. For business, for women's rights, for my relationship with my life partner."

"Who is a woman?"

"Yes. Natalie"

"Natalie what?"

"Goddard. She has taken my name."

"She live with you?"

"No. We do not wish to reconstruct the same narrowly defining box that too many of our married sisters have been enclosed by."

"Where's she live?"

"She has an apartment on Revere Street."

"She know about Lawrence?"

"No."

"Tell me about him."

"I am, in all ways, philosophically, socially, politically, a lesbian. My—for lack of a better word—my biology has betrayed me. Biologically, I am bisexual. Now and then I need sex with a man."

"And Lawrence B. Reeves was the most recent."

"Yes."

"There have been others."

"Yes. They never knew my name, nor I theirs."

"Pick them up in bars or wherever?"

"Yes. I am not a terribly handsome woman. But I am not choosy, and there is a certain kind of man that finds me desirable. Perhaps I remind them of their mothers."

"But Lawrence was different?"

"Yes. For one thing, he knew who I was. I don't know how, exactly. He may have seen me lecture, or read about me in the newspapers. By now my profile has become perhaps too high to be picking people up in bars."

"You saw him more than once?"

"Yes. He wasn't handsome, nor was he particularly accomplished. But he was sexually adroit, and he was educated. He could talk about ideas, which I rather liked in him. We were discreet. We went to the suburbs. Lawrence would check in and I would join him later. No one ever saw me."

"So what happened?"

"He wanted more than I could offer. He

seemed infatuated. Flowers. Phone calls. Natalie was beginning to ask about the bouquets that were filling my home. After several evenings, I told him I wouldn't be able to see him again. He was furious. Told me I was a bitch, the all-purpose male pejorative."

My experience with men suggested that they had a lot stronger pejoratives than that, but I wasn't here to argue.

"And?" I said.

"And he began to harass me. Phone calls at first. Then when I had my number changed, letters."

"Abusive?"

"Yes. Obscene and violent."

"For instance?"

She shook her head. "It's too distasteful."

"You keep any?"

"No. After a time, I began to return his letters unopened. At which point he began to follow me, and I hired you."

"Do you think Lawrence hired someone to kill you?" I said.

"He was capable of anything."

"In his rage," I said, "and, apparently the owner of a loaded handgun, wouldn't he have been more likely to do it himself?"

"I don't know. I know he was not normal."

"Do you think, having hired a killer, and having the killer get the wrong woman, Lawrence would have put a gun in his mouth and blown the top of his head off?"

She shivered, her hands still tented in front of her.

"I don't know," she said.

She dropped her head and pressed her tented hands against her forehead. The movement looked a little rehearsed to me.

"God, if only I hadn't. I'm so ashamed. I hate that part of me. It's like an itch that has to be scratched."

She raised her head and looked at me. That movement, too, looked practiced.

"What must you think of me?" she said.

"What if Lawrence didn't hire somebody to kill you," I said.

"He confessed to doing that," she said.

"Just for a fresh perspective. What if somebody wanted to kill Gretchen. Who might that be?"

"That's absurd. No one would want to kill Gretchen. It was obviously somebody wanting to kill me."

"Would you mind if I browsed through her files, see what she was doing professionally?"

"Can we keep my relationship to Lawrence between us?"

Give something. Get something.

"I have no current need to share it with anyone," I said.

"I think you are wasting your time, but you are free to investigate Gretchen to your heart's content," Mary Lou said.

CHAPTER

26

I SAT IN Gretchen Crane's cubicle for most of the day. Somehow the absence of human occupancy made even so sterile an environment as this tiny office seem emptier than was reasonable. Stillness seemed to have permeated it. I went systematically through her file cabinet. I nosed about in her computer. There were lists of names of women who'd been ill treated in one way or another, cataloged by the nature of the mistreatment: Domestic Abuse. Workplace Harassment. Folders like that. There were lists of laws, cataloged by state, that seemed in one way or another repressive to women. There were the names of public figures, noting their position on various women's issues, and lists of legislators and their voting record on legislation relating to women. There was a collection of sexist jokes. There was a large folder of stuff on prostitution as the embodiment of sexism, where the whores were little more than chattel. There was a plan for a prostitutes' union, with a note: *See Home File*. There were clippings of news-

125

paper and magazine pieces, apparently sexist in content.

The massive collection of stuff was beginning, by late afternoon, to make me paranoid. I knew sexism existed, and I knew, since she was the company researcher, that it was one of Gretchen Crane's jobs to collect evidence of it. But if I felt paranoid after an afternoon of reading, how must she have felt? How must Mary Lou feel, when she wasn't scratching her itch? I knew a lot of sexists, which often played to my advantage because men would underestimate me. I also knew a lot of men who were not sexist. I knew several men for whom a woman was, and had been most of their life, their best friend, their partner, their counselor, and the center of their existence. Richie was like that in many ways. Too much so, maybe. Maybe he and I could have used a little sexism. And I remembered Mary Lou's reaction to my Rosie when she'd first met her. Blatant dogism.

There was another thing. I had found a host of stuff about sexism. I had found absolutely nothing about Gretchen. There was nothing personal in her files. There were no pictures on her desk. No indication that she had any life beyond the encapsulated life she lived in this cubicle, where she researched the bad things that happened to women. Was her life in fact so barren, or was she just one who compartmentalized?

I went into Mary Lou's office and asked her. "Other than in the workplace," Mary Lou said, "I know nothing about Gretchen. She was, I believe, married once, but that ended before she began work here."

"Home address?"

She gave it to me.

"How about the ex-husband? Know his name?"

"No."

"Could it be Crane?"

"I doubt that someone as enlightened as Gretchen would keep her ex-husband's name."

"Probably not. You wouldn't know where he lives, would you?"

"No. And I still can't understand why you are interested."

"I don't think Lawrence Reeves killed himself," I said. "That thought calls all in doubt."

"And why do you have this peculiar skepticism, again?"

"He didn't have ammunition for the gun that killed him. I've never heard of anyone buying a gun without buying a box of ammunition. But say he did, the gun was loaded, would he have run out and bought six bullets? There's no record of a gun permit, which would be necessary to buy a gun, or ammunition, in this state. He wasn't the kind of man who'd own a gun. He wasn't the kind of man who would know how to hire a hit man, and, I'm sorry, I don't think he was the kind of man to kill himself."

"You don't know him well enough to make these judgments," Mary Lou said.

"Absolutely," I said. "Nor do I know him well enough to decide that he would own a gun and know a hit man and kill himself. But they are judgments that have to be made; either he did it, or he didn't, and there's enough that's bothersome about the hypothesis that he did, to make me at least consider that he didn't."

"Well, I won't begrudge you your logic."

"Thanks. And if that holds, it follows that maybe somebody else killed Gretchen, and maybe intended to. In which case perhaps the answer lies in her life, not yours."

"And why aren't the police thinking this way?"

"Because they have approximately skady-eight other cases to think about, and if one closes itself neatly, they don't have time to bother it."

"But you do."

"Yes."

"Well, I think you are entirely wrong," Mary Lou said. "But I admire your thirst for justice."

"Or whatever," I said.

"Or whatever."

CHAPTER

27

GRETCHEN LIVED IN an apartment complex off of Route 28 in Stoneham. I told the super that I was from Gretchen's office and needed to see if there was any work of hers that she had taken home and that needed to be returned. He nodded sympathetically and let me into Gretchen's apartment.

"This will take a while," I said.

"Sure," he said. "Just pull the door shut when you leave. It locks automatically."

"I will."

I looked around. More than in her office, the silence of her apartment was heavy. It was as if it were pressing in on me. The walls of the three-room apartment were painted white. Nothing hung on them: no paintings, no imported tapestries, no movie posters, no photographs of anyone, no mirrors, except for the one on the medicine cabinet door in the bathroom.

The place was furnished in early monastic. The living room had a beige-colored couch with maple arms, a square table painted white with four white straight chairs set around it, and a personal computer on the table in front of one of the chairs, with a printer underneath the table. The bedroom contained a single bed, made up with white linens and an army blanket, and on the wall opposite, a cheap pine bureau painted white.

The bathroom was white tile, a white toilet, a white stand-alone sink, a white tub with a white shower curtain, and a white medicine cabinet with the mirrored door. Gretchen had not been a flamboyant girl. In the medicine cabinet she kept a toothbrush and a tube of toothpaste, rolled up carefully from the bottom. There was a bottle of rubbing alcohol in there as well, and a package of gum stimulators. Her closet had three of what my grandmother had called housedresses, and there was a shoe rack on the floor with one pair of thick-soled walking shoes on it. Her bureau had some Tampax, five white tee shirts, several pairs of thin white socks, two pairs of jeans, and some functional underwear. There was far too much room for more in both her closet and her bureau. Between us Gretchen and I probably averaged out about right.

Her refrigerator had a half a loaf of seven-grain bread, and a quart of milk that had turned sour. In the freezer were several frozen vegetarian dinners, and a package of frozen soy-based imitation hamburgers. There was no booze in the house. There was in fact nothing in the house that suggested a life lived with exhilaration.

I went back into the living room and sat at

her table and turned on her computer. I was not the queen of cyberspace, but I had the same kind of computer she did and I had mastered rudiments like turning it on. I looked around in her hard drive for a while and found very little. A shopping list, a bank-by-mail setup that required a password, an AOL connection, password again, a folder marked *Addresses, Contacts, etc.*, and a folder marked *Mail.* I opened the mail folder and read copies of letters she had sent. They told me nothing, except that Gretchen had a sister living in Toronto. I tried *Addresses, Contacts, etc.* This seemed a catchall. Mary Lou Goddard's address and phone were in there, work and office; and a number of other people who I assumed were colleagues. Many of them had the same office address as Mary Lou. There was nothing special about any of the addresses except one name and number that I knew: Sgt. Robert Franco, who was a vice detective. The number was Boston Police Headquarters. The name went with the rest of her addresses like schmaltz herring on a cupcake. I sat for a while looking at the name. Was I confronted with a clue? I reached under the table and switched on Gretchen's printer and ran off her one-page list of addresses. Then I shut everything off, put the list in my purse, and left. The door shut behind me and locked automatically.

CHAPTER

28

I MET BOBBY Franco for coffee in a diner on Mass Avenue near the corner of Magazine Street in Roxbury. He was a little round guy, not much taller than I am, kind of cute, with a bald head and a thin moustache and a nice smile. When I came in he stood up from where he was sitting at the counter.

"Sunny Randall," he said.

He was wearing small sunglasses, jeans, work boots, and a gray sweatshirt under a red VFW baseball jacket, the sweatshirt hood hanging out over the collar. Vice cops take pride in dressing down.

I sat on a stool at the counter beside him and ordered tea.

"Have some pie with that," Bobby said.

"Pie?" I said. "Are you out of your mind? If I sat here and ate pie with you, my jeans would be too tight when I stood up."

"I was hoping," Bobby said.

"Sure you were, you're the most married guy I ever knew."

"Doesn't mean I don't notice," Bobby said.

My tea arrived and fresh coffee for Bobby.

"The reason I called," I said, "was that I have your name on a list of addresses I took from the apartment of Gretchen Crane, who was recently shot to death."

"Crane?"

"Yes, Gretchen Crane. Worked for a company called Great Strides. She was shot to death a week or so ago. Homicide has concluded it was a case of mistaken identity."

"You don't think so?"

"I don't know. The best part about their theory is that it clears a couple of cases at once."

"Command staff always admires that," Bobby said.

"I don't care about command staff anymore," I said.

"That's nice. How is it out there in private practice?"

"No command staff," I said.

"Not much of a pension either."

"Nothing's perfect," I said. "Do you know Gretchen Crane?"

"Yeah. Odd woman."

"Probably," I said. "Why does she have your name and number?"

"I think she got it from some writer at the *Globe*," Bobby said. "She called and made an appointment and came out to Roxbury to see me. You know her?"

"The only time I ever saw her she was dead."

"Hard to really know someone you meet that way," Bobby said.

In front of us, the counterwoman put a slab of pie on a plate and carried it down to the other end of the diner and gave it to a thick black man.

"Is that cherry pie?" Bobby said to the counterwoman.

"Sure."

"I better have some," Bobby said.

"Sure."

She put the pie on a plate and put it in front of Bobby with a fork. He took a bite.

"By God," he said, "it is cherry."

"I'm happy for you," I said. "Gretchen Crane."

"Very serious woman." Bobby sipped a little coffee. "Wanted my views on prostitution."

"Why?"

"Some kind of a research project."

"What did you do?"

"I let her ride with me, couple days. Introduced her around. She wanted to know if there was any kind of, how did she say, vertical integration in prostitution."

"Vertical integration?"

"Yeah. I thought it was a position, but she said no. She said she was interested in who ran prostitution. She's talking chain of command."

"That assumes more organization than I ever knew about," I said.

"It does," Bobby said. "She says she heard the top guy is Tony Marcus. And I say, far as I know."

"And?"

"And she says she has an appointment with him. And I said he was no one for a woman like her to be chatting with. She said I was guilty of sexism, and wouldn't have said that if she were a man."

"Which you would have."

"Yeah, of course. Tony Marcus is no one to be chatting with, male or female, unless you're a cop."

"I agree."

"Do I seem sexist to you, Sweet Cakes?"

"Deeply," I said.

"Anyway, I gave Tony a jingle, said she was coming by, just to make sure."

"Is he still in the same place?"

"Yep, Buddy's Fox, in the South End."

"I know where it is."

"You going to talk with him?"

"Yes."

"Want me to come along?" Bobby said.

"I appreciate the offer, you sexist bastard, but no thank you."

"You going to pay for the pie and coffee?" Bobby said.

"That's man's work," I said.

CHAPTER

29

JULIE SAT AT my kitchen counter, in the late afternoon, her face pinched, her eyes puffy, and drank a bourbon and water.

"I wish I smoked," she said.

"Trying for every vice?" I said.

"What's that mean?"

"You're drinking a lot."

"So what?"

"Just a little light banter," I said. "You look miserable."

"I am."

"What can I do?"

"You can come with me while I get an abortion."

"You're pregnant?"

Julie drank some bourbon. Rosie raised her head from my bed where she was sleeping at the other end of the loft. She looked for signs of food associated with the clinking of ice in a glass, saw that there was none, and put her head back down.

"That would probably be the basis for an abortion," she said.

"Dumb response," I said. "Sorry."

"It's okay. I don't know what the smart response would have been."

"Maybe a quiet nod."

"Maybe."

We sat in silence.

"Can I have another splash?" Julie said.

I got up and got her more bourbon.

"How about Michael?" I said.

"He doesn't know."

"Is it his?"

Julie drank some more.

"No."

"Do we know whose it is?"

"Probably Robert."

"Does he know?"

"No."

"Do you think he should?" I said.

"There's probably a time for us to talk about what I'm doing with my life," Julie said. "But right now I don't need you to be Jiminy Cricket, Sunny. I am going to get an abortion and I'm terrified to go alone."

"Of course," I said. "I'll go with you."

On my bed, Rosie made a couple of small dog sounds in her sleep. Julie looked into her glass for a moment before she drank.

"I never thought I'd become this," she said. "I always thought I'd marry a nice man and raise my children and work part-time helping people solve their problems, and sink into a happy routine with the man I loved. Maybe travel a little when the kids were grown."

"I never thought I'd be divorced," I said.

"Life does it to you, doesn't it," Julie said.

"I'm not sure it's life's fault," I said.

"Oh for God's sake, Sunny, have a drink, and wallow with me."

I got myself a glass of white wine, and sat back down beside Julie at the counter.

"That's better," Julie said. "The thing is I like Michael. I probably love him a little."

"Probably?"

"Probably."

"I think love is pretty certain."

"That's because you're you, Sunny. Things are very clear for you. You know who you are. You know what you want, and it's what you should want. You like your dog. You do your work."

"I love my dog," I said.

"See what I mean? Nice and clear."

"Except I love Richie and we're divorced."

"Shit happens," Julie said. "But you haven't panicked. You haven't gotten yourself knocked up by some guy you don't care about."

"I know what I want," I said.

Julie poured herself some more bourbon and added ice. She didn't bother with the water this time.

"I do too," she said. "I want to do whatever I want to do, and not be disapproved of all the fucking time."

"Michael disapproves of you?"

"He thinks I'm not a good mother, and he thinks I'm not...he thinks I'm not very good in bed."

"Are you?"

"With him? No."

"And he pressures you about it."

"Yes. Bad mother, bad wife."

"And the more he pressures you?"

"The worse I am in bed."

"And the music goes round and round...," I said.

Julie patted her still-flat stomach. "And it comes out here," she said.

CHAPTER

30

AT MIDMORNING, I sat in a booth near the bar in Buddy's Fox with a dissipated-looking black man named Tony Marcus, who dressed very well, and was quite handsome in a lax sort of way. His bodyguard, a huge man named Junior, took up most of the bar across the back, and his personal shooter, a thin black boy named Ty-Bop, jittered aimlessly near the front door. The restaurant was about half full. I was the only white person there. Tony was having breakfast.

"So," Tony said, "Sunny Randall, on the job again."

"This one is sort of pro bono, Tony."

"I hate pro bono," Tony said. "You want some eggs?"

"No, thank you," I said. "I've had breakfast."

"Up and at 'em Sunny Randall. What do you want from me?"

"You ever talk with a woman named Gretchen Crane?"

"Why you want to know?" Tony said.

He was having scrambled eggs and onions, and he was very delicate in putting a small bite into his mouth, and patting his lips with his napkin afterwards.

"She was killed last week."

"And you're on it?"

"Sort of."

"You got a client?"

"Not at the moment."

"Gretchen Crane a friend of yours."

"I never met her."

"So why you care what happened to her?"

"You have to care about something," I said.

"You still got that funny-looking dog?" Tony said.

"No. I have Rosie."

"One looks like Spuds McKenzie in the beer ads?"

"Yes."

"That's the one," Tony said. "Care about her."

I reached across the booth and took a triangle of toast off of Tony's plate and nibbled on it. Butter! I hadn't had butter on toast since childhood.

"Does this mean you won't comment on Gretchen Crane?" I said.

"No."

I had another bite of toast.

"She come to see me two-three weeks ago. Cop I know sent her over."

"Bobby Franco."

"Yeah. Anyway, she was real serious. Real

worried about how black folks don't get a break. Real interested in prostitution."

"In what way was she interested?"

"Wanted to know mostly how it worked, how the whores got treated, how the business was organized. I told her whores got treated like whores, and the business was organized to make money for me."

"How'd that work for her?"

"Hey, she talking to a black gangster, I didn't talk like that she be heartbroken," Tony said.

"Did you tell her anything else?"

Tony finished his eggs. The last bite of eggs was balanced by a last bite of onions, and a last triangle of toast. Tony was very orderly.

"Not much. I get bored pretty quick talking to high-toned white ladies. I sent her to see Jermaine."

"Who's Jermaine?" I said.

"Jermaine Lister. He runs the whores for me."

"You're letting people run things for you?"

"You get too big after a while to do it all yourself. You try and somebody starts biting off a corner while you busy with something else."

"Gee," I said. "Sort of like organized crime."

Tony grinned.

"Sort of," he said.

"Did she talk to Jermaine?"

"Don't know."

"Wouldn't he tell you?"

"You do business right, you put people in charge, and you leave them alone. Unless they fuck up."

"And then?"

"Then Ty-Bop downsizes them," Tony said and smiled widely. "You want to talk with Jermaine?"

"Yes."

"Junior," Tony said without bothering to look. "Call Jermaine, tell him Sunny Randall's coming over. Tell him she's okay, long as she don't nose into our business."

Junior reached behind the bar and pulled up a phone.

"How come you're so helpful?" I said. "I'm on the other side. If I could bust you I would."

"I know that, but you're fun, Sunny Randall. You're good-looking and you got a lot of balls."

"You sweet-talking devil," I said.

"I like to see what you going to do."

"And if I nose into your business?" I said.

"Then Ty-Bop be downsizing you."

CHAPTER

31

JULIE PICKED ME up at 8:30 and we drove to Brighton to the clinic. There were a few scraggly-looking protesters trudging around outside. None of them looked like they were ever likely to be pregnant.

"You want to go in?" I said.

"Not yet," Julie said. "My appointment's not till nine. I hate sitting in the waiting room looking at the other women like me."

"We can sit in the car," I said.

Julie stared at the protesters.

"Do you think they'll bother us when we go in?"

"They might call you a murderer or something," I said. "They don't look very energetic."

"I hope no one has a bomb," Julie said.

"They probably don't," I said.

"Remember a few years ago somebody shot up a clinic?"

"Yes."

"Do you have a gun, Sunny?"

"I always have a gun. But I doubt that I'll need it."

We were quiet as Julie stared at the pickets.

"Are you clear with yourself," I said, "that you want to do this?"

"I have to do it."

"Okay. Then stop scaring yourself to death about it. It is a routine medical procedure. It happens every day. You don't need to punish yourself in advance."

"Do you think this is right?"

"For you? Not for me to say."

"If you were me, would you do this?"

"I think you've made some mistakes that I hope I wouldn't make. But if I had and was where you are? Yes, I'd do this."

"What do you think about abortion generally?" Julie said.

She was nervous. Her face was pale under her makeup, which made the makeup garish. She swallowed frequently.

"I try not to spend too much time thinking about things generally," I said.

"But you must sometimes."

"Generally I think there are absolutely compelling arguments on both sides of the issue."

"So how does one resolve it?"

"One does what one must."

"Without knowing if it's right?"

"Knowing it's right for you at the moment."

"That sounds dangerously like situational ethics," Julie said.

"Probably is," I said.

I looked at the clock on the dashboard.

"Time," I said.

"Oh, Jesus," Julie said.

"It's just another visit to the gyno," I said. "I'll stay right with you."

"I can't think. I don't know."

"Julie," I said. "If you do this, when it's over you'll have defined your view on abortion. Which is that it's necessary, under certain circumstances, at certain times."

"Sunny..."

I waited. She didn't move. There were tears in her eyes, and her breathing was shallow and fast.

"If I could tell you what to do, I would," I said. "I wish I could. But I know this: We can leave, but the problem won't. And it becomes more of a problem every day."

"'It,'" she said.

I was quiet. I had nothing left to say. I looked at the straggle of pickets. Anybody have a gun? I unzipped the belly pack where I was carrying mine. Julie opened the door and got out of the car. I got out on my side and we walked across the street toward the clinic. A short fat old man with a fringe of gray hair muttered, "Butchers," as we walked past him. I had the impulse to yell, *not me,* which I had the grace to suppress as we walked through the door to the clinic.

CHAPTER

32

BEING IN RICHIE'S apartment always made
me think about how fully he was embodied by
where he lived. Everything that he needed
was there, and each thing was where it should
be. But there was nothing extra. Nothing
ornamental. Nothing that was there simply to
be attractive. When I let myself in, Richie
was having a drink with Rosie. They were on
the couch with Rosie lying beside him, her chin
resting on his thigh. Opening his door with my
key, seeing him with his feet up and our dog
sleeping beside him made a surge of hot
domesticity flood through me. Safety. Refuge.
Certainty. Home.

Rosie's head shot up. Her ears bent slightly
forward. She stared at me while the small brain
adjusted to my presence. Then she jumped down
and ran over and turned around a number of
times while I crouched down to greet her. Richie
stood holding his drink and smiled while Rosie
and I reconnected. When we had, I stood up
and he opened his arms and I went and kissed
him. More than sister. Less than wife.

"Want a drink?"

"Yes. What are you drinking?"

"Scotch and soda."

"That sounds good," I said.

Richie made me a drink and freshened his and we sat on the couch with Rosie between us and put our feet up on the big hassock in front. I took the first drink and let it ease into me. I was not much of a drinker, but there were moments when nothing seemed quite as perfect as a strong drink with a lot of ice.

"She been good?" I said, looking down at Rosie, who was in a paroxysm of contentment between us.

"Sure. She loves me. Even if she doesn't live here," Richie said.

"Not unlike myself."

"Not unlike."

We each drank a little of our drinks.

"You went to see Tony Marcus."

"How do you know?" I said.

Richie shrugged like he does. It was a shrug that said, in effect, I know stuff.

I said, "You don't have anyone looking out for me? Do you?"

"Like who?" he said.

"You know damn well like who. Your father or your uncle would have somebody to keep an eye on me. All you'd have to do is ask."

"I know you wouldn't like that," Richie said.

I nodded. We were quiet.

"You haven't exactly answered my question," I said.

"No. I'm not having anyone look out for you."

"But you knew about Tony."

Richie grinned at me.

"Maybe my family is keeping track of Tony," he said.

I laughed.

"You mean it's not all about me?"

"Not always," Richie said.

"How disheartening," I said.

"Was Tony helpful?"

I told him.

"Jermaine Lister," Richie said when I was through.

"Yes. Do you know him?"

"Yes."

"And?"

"And I don't push into your business without being invited."

"You're invited," I said.

"He's a vicious stupid pimp," Richie said, "that Tony promoted to the level of his incompetence."

"Why would Tony do that?"

"Hard to figure about Tony. He does what he feels like doing because it amuses him, and if he makes a mistake, he just erases it."

"So he knows Jermaine is incompetent."

"Oh yeah."

"And he promoted him to watch him flounder? That doesn't make any sense."

"Well, my uncle says that Jermaine wants to replace Tony, and has wanted to for a while. So Tony promotes him so he's reporting to Tony regularly. It's sort of a way to watch him."

"Why wouldn't Tony just kill him?"

"Tony is Tony. He's playful. He does stuff because he wants to see what will happen."

"Like me."

"Yeah. He likes you. Doesn't mean he wouldn't kill you. But as long as you aren't interfering with business, he likes to watch what you'll do. He's never seen a woman like you."

"Gee, Tony likes me."

"Ain't it flattering."

"You think Jermaine will like me?"

"No."

"Because?"

"Because Jermaine doesn't like anything that I know of. And he especially doesn't like women."

"Which is why Tony sent me to him," I said.

Richie smiled.

"He got a big boot out of it when I took someone away from one of his pimps last year," I said.

Richie nodded.

"And he's moving me up a notch, see what I can do against Jermaine."

"You should be flattered," Richie said. "Tony's treating you like a contender. Why do you need to talk with Jermaine?"

"I'm following the path of a woman who was murdered. She talked with Tony, and he sent her to Jermaine."

"And now she's dead," Richie said.

"Yes."

"Good to keep that in mind," he said.

My drink was gone. I rattled the ice in the empty glass and Richie got up and made us each another one.

"I could of course trail along when you talk with him."

I shook my head.

"Spike?" Richie said.

I shook my head again.

Richie nodded, more to himself than to me.

"Have you ever seen a woman like me?" I said.

"No."

"How do you feel about that?"

"Sometimes I wish there were dozens," Richie said. "Then I could marry one of them and stop mooning over you."

"Would you actually like to be married again?"

"I like monogamy," Richie said. "I don't like to share you."

"I have feelings for you that I don't have for anyone else," I said.

"I know. It's a kind of exclusivity," Richie said.

"It's the only kind I am capable of right now."

"I know that too."

"And I appreciate it that you don't insist," I said.

Richie smiled.

"I can't insist," Richie said. "You won't do it."

"It's too…" I fumbled for the right word. "It's too possessory," I said. "I don't say forever, but right now. I'm not…there's still not enough of me to be exclusively yours."

"I know."

"Dating other men is a way to remind myself that I'm not exclusively anyone's."

"I know that, Sunny. I know all of it. I don't like all of it. But I'm in this for the long haul."

"I can't promise it will work out the way you want it," I said.

"If it doesn't it doesn't. But I'm not going to quit on it. If you don't want to see me anymore and you're clear on it, say so and I'll get on with my life."

"I can't say that. I don't think I'll ever say that."

"Then I won't quit."

I leaned across Rosie and laid my head on Richie's shoulder.

"I'm sorry I'm this way," I said.

Richie put his arm around me. Rosie looked up from between us. If she had the face for it, I think she would have frowned.

"There's no point to that," Richie said.

I nodded against his shoulder. He bumped the top of my head lightly with his jaw. Rosie squirmed into a more comfortable position on the couch between us.

"We could make love," I said.

"That's always good," Richie said.

Which it was.

CHAPTER

33

I HAD JUST fed Rosie her supper when Hal Reagan called me.

"Sunny," he said. "Come get your god-damned sister."

"Hi, Hal," I said. "How nice of you to call."

"She stole my car and hid it somewhere. And she is making a scene."

"Call the cops," I said.

"How would your mother and father feel about that? Their daughter arrested. How would you feel? You need to get over here."

Actually I would feel quite good about Elizabeth in jail.

"Where is here?"

"The Coach House in Sudbury."

"On the Post Road?"

"Yes."

"Okay. It'll take me about forty-five minutes."

"Just come as fast as you can."

"Sure," I said.

Driving out Route 20 I thought of that line from Robert Frost: *Home is where when you have to go there, they have to take you in.* It was as close as I could get to explaining why I didn't say the hell with Elizabeth. I didn't even like Elizabeth. And I was missing my night class on Low Country Realism.

I found myself stuck behind someone who was going just faster than a dead stop and I didn't get there until nearly 8:30. The Coach House is one of those suburban restaurants that pretends to offer an authentic eighteenth-century dining experience. It was sided in dark-stained board and batten. It had a wood shingle roof, or, at least, a roof shingled in something that looked like wood. It had a porte-cochère out front, and leaded windows. The menu featured stuff like pot roast and shepherd's pie, and beer served in pewter tankards. The waitresses wore long dresses and aprons.

The dining room had a bar near the door, and oak tables around the room. At about half of them, people were dining. At one of them Hal Reagan was sitting grimly with Nancy Simpson. Both had their coats on. Neither was saying anything to the other. At the end of the bar nearest the door was Elizabeth wearing a long black coat with a fur collar over pink sweats and white running shoes. Her purse sat on the bar beside her. As soon as I came in, I could tell that she was drunk. Her eyes had that soft look around them that they always developed. On the bar in front of her was a low ball glass of something clear with ice in it. I went

154

straight to the bar and picked up her purse and took her car keys out and pocketed them.

"Sunny? What the hell...?"

I put her purse on the bar.

"I'm going to give them a ride home, then I'll come back and get you," I said.

"Tha' bastard called you," she said.

"Yep. It was me or the cops."

"Let him walk, the son'va bitch. Let his whore walk."

"Hal," I said. "Come on. I'll drive you home."

"What about my car?"

"Police will find it someplace. Let's go."

"How am I going to get to work in the morning?" Hal said.

He was on his feet now, standing behind me, so that I was a buffer between him and Elizabeth.

"Borrow hers," I said and nodded at Nancy, who stood behind him double-buffered.

"And how is she supposed to get around?"

"Hal. Life's imperfect. Sometimes stopgap measures are all there are."

"So she gets away with this."

"Goddamn it, Hal. You called me. I didn't call you. Either do what I say or I'll go home, and you can work this out among the three of you."

"No. You can drive us home."

"Thank you. Elizabeth, stay here. I'll be back for you."

"She's drunk," I said to the bartender. "Don't give her another drink." He shrugged.

"You can't drive them," Elizabeth said.

"Sit still," I said.

Elizabeth slid off the stool and stood in the doorway.

"You're not goin' anywhere," she said.

As soon as she got off her stool, the bartender quietly picked up her drink and threw it away. I stepped close to my sister and wrapped my arms around her and pinned her arms to her sides. Then I pushed her against the doorjamb.

"Green Subaru wagon," I said. "Parked in the no-parking zone right out front. It's not locked. I'll be there in a second."

Elizabeth said, "Le' go of me, you bitch."

I held her against the doorjamb as Hal and Nancy scooted past us. Elizabeth kicked me in the ankle, but since she was wearing sneakers it didn't hurt as much as it might have.

"Whore," Elizabeth shouted.

"Listen," I said.

"Fucking whore!"

I banged her against the doorjamb.

"Listen to me, or I'll hit you."

"Hit me?"

"You are making a perfect asshole of yourself," I said. "You're too drunk to drive yourself home. Shut up and sit here and wait for me to come get you."

"I don't care," she said. "I don't care about anything."

She looked out the doorway where Hal and Nancy had gone. She said "whoremonger" loudly.

I pulled out all the stops.

"You do what I say or I'll call Daddy."

Her head snapped around.

"You're not going to tell on me?"

Bingo!

"Not if you do what I say."

"I don't want Daddy to know."

"Sit there," I said and turned her toward the bar stool and let her go. It took her two tries to get her butt back up on the stool. The bartender promptly put her bill on the bar before her. I turned and headed for my car.

The ride to Weston was Gothic.

"Go to Nancy's place," Hal said when I got in the car.

"Okay," I said. "You notify the local police that your car is stolen. It'll turn up someplace and they'll call you. I assume you have spare keys."

"Yes."

No other words were spoken until I let them out in Weston.

Hal said, "Thank you."

I said, "Sure," and headed back to Sudbury.

When I walked back into the Coach House, there was no sign of Elizabeth.

"She walked out," the bartender said. "Left a thirty-two-dollar bar tab."

I gave him a credit card. He imprinted it and gave me the charge slip. I overtipped him, and signed it.

"Sorry for the trouble," I said.

"No problem," he said.

I found Elizabeth walking along the Post Road about twenty minutes later. I pulled up beside her and opened the window on her side and said, "Get in." She shook her head.

I said, "Elizabeth, get in the goddamned car or I will get out and throw you in."

She walked maybe two more steps. I eased the car alongside her again.

"In," I said.

She opened the passenger door and got in. She was crying.

"I'm cold," she said.

I rolled up the window on the passenger side.

"Heat," she said, "I need heat."

"Heater's on," I said. "You'll be warm in a minute."

We rode in silence, Elizabeth staring straight ahead at the center stripe unspooling in the headlights. Finally I spoke.

"If you were cold, why didn't you button up your coat?" I said.

She kept staring at the road.

"What's the difference," she said.

"Maybe you wanted to be cold."

"That's ridiculous."

"Maybe it was who you are at the moment— out in the cold."

"What?"

One had to go slowly with Elizabeth.

"The way people act is often, ah, symbolic of how they feel."

I knew *symbolic* was risky.

"I feel just fine."

"No you don't," I said. "You feel rejected and embarrassed and humiliated and unloved and unlovely and frightened and alone and God knows what else, just as I would in your position."

"As soon as he saw me come in, the bastard, he got right up and left. You should have seen his face when he came back in because his car was missing."

A car came up on us from the opposite direction. Its headlights illuminated us for a moment and then it passed and we were in the dark again following the narrow channel of my headlights.

"And what did you get out of all that?" I said.

"I showed the sonofabitch."

"What did you show him?"

"I showed him he can't cheat on me and get away with it."

"Elizabeth. He does cheat on you. In your definition he is cheating on you as we speak. He's home in bed with another woman. You're walking along the highway in the cold half gassed and freezing your ass."

She began to cry.

"And crying," I said.

"What do you want me to do?" she said between sobs. "Just let him walk over me?"

"Maybe you shouldn't be thinking of it in terms of who walks over who," I said. "Maybe you shouldn't be deciding things in terms of its impact on him?"

"What?"

"Maybe you should be thinking about your best interest," I said.

"Sure. And my best interest is to be alone and nearly forty with no money and no job and no skills and no husband."

"Have you been enjoying life lately?" I said.

"You know it's been hell for me."

"So if being married and having your husband support you is hell, what have you got to lose by trying another approach?"

She cried for a little while without speaking, but finally she said, "I can't. I don't know how."

"I can put you in touch with people who will help you."

"You mean a shrink."

"Yes."

"I'm not having some crazy Jew poking into my private life."

I breathed for a while. Elizabeth cried.

"I know these are hard times. Everybody's pretty nutty when the relationship goes south. But when the nuttiness subsides, you will have to grow up and begin to think about things the way grown-ups do. I can't force you to look out for yourself. And I can't look out for you. All I'm asking now is that you try not to make any significant decisions while you're crazy. Just try to hold on to yourself. We're not so close. But you're my sister. I'll help you any way I can."

We turned onto Elizabeth's street in silence. I parked in front of her house.

"You want me to come in?" I said.

She shook her head.

"You won't tell Daddy," she said.

I sighed.

"No," I said. "I won't tell Daddy."

She nodded and got out and walked to her house and went in.

CHAPTER

34

THE DAY STARTED out with a dark threat of rain. I wore my efficient-looking silver trench coat. Before I left, I got two one-hundred-dollar bills from my bank. Hundreds are very effective for bribing people. I found Jermaine Lister on Columbus Ave, near the corner of Mass Ave, leaning on the right front fender of the biggest Mercedes made. The car was silver-colored and had tinted windows. Jermaine was wearing a belted Harris tweed overcoat and a dark brown scally cap. There were several whores in a group talking with him when I showed up, rounding the corner from Mass Avenue where I'd parked my Subaru. The whores looked at me balefully.

"Jermaine Lister?" I said.

He nodded once.

"Sunny Randall."

He nodded again.

"Tony Marcus sent me to see you."

Nod.

"Did you know a woman named Gretchen Crane?"

"White broad?"

"Yes."

"Sure. Tony sent her along to me just like he did you."

"What was her interest?"

"She wanted to find out all about pros-ti-tu-tion," Jermaine said.

"Why?"

"Maybe thinking about a career," Jermaine said and winked at the whores. They giggled. "You want to find out 'bout it? You'd make a lot more money than Gretchen."

"Oh golly," I said. "What kinds of questions did she ask?"

"Don't know. I turned her over to my, ah, staff."

Jermaine winked at the whores again. They giggled again.

"Any of your staff here?" I said.

The tallest of the girls looked at Jermaine.

"Nope," Jermaine said.

"Where can I find someone who talked with Gretchen?"

"Don't really know," Jermaine said. "You ladies of the evening know?"

They giggled again. No one admitted knowing. Jermaine's beeper went off. He checked it.

" 'Scuse me," he said and took out a cell phone and dialed. He listened, then he said, "This is J," and listened again. He looked at me while he listened, then moved away so I couldn't hear him and said a couple of words and clicked off the cell phone.

"Can't never get away from business," he said. "Where were we?"

"You were telling me how you sent Gretchen to talk with some hookers but you don't know which ones?"

"This here is a fluid business," Jermaine said. "Ladies come. They go. These ladies went. Can't help you."

"Gee, Tony said you might."

"I'm trying," Jermaine said. "But I don't know nothing."

"Well thanks for trying," I said.

"Sho' nuff," Jermaine said.

The whores giggled. I went back up Mass Ave.

I was parked far enough up Mass Ave toward Huntington that I was out of their sight when I got in the car. I pulled away from the curb and went down Huntington to Copley Place, turned right onto Dartmouth and right again on Columbus and parked at a hydrant with a view of the Mass Ave corner. Jermaine's car was there for maybe an hour before it pulled away and cruised on down Columbus to visit some of his other retail sites. I took my hundred-dollar bill from my purse, and folded it long so you could see the denomination. Then I got out and walked up to the same corner I'd been on, where the same whores were still clustered.

I had my folded hundred in my hand. A small part of my brain was wondering why everyone, me included, folded a bill before duking somebody.

"Could I buy a few minutes of your time?"
I said to the tall whore who'd exchanged a
glance with Jermaine.

"I don't do women," she said.

"Me either," I said. "Just a cup of coffee and
a little chitchat."

The tall whore looked at the $100.

"Sure," she said. "Got to stay 'round here
though. I'm waiting for somebody."

"Okay." I leaned on the wall beside her, tap-
ping the folded bill on my thigh.

"Shoo," the tall whore said to the aimless
little gathering of other whores. "I got to talk
with this lady."

They moved away. They seemed restless, and
a little tense, as if there were something to come.

"My name is Sunny," I said.

"Jewell," the tall whore said.

She wasn't looking at me. She was restless, looking at the street. She seemed edgy.
Was she worried about Jermaine? If so, why
wouldn't she get off the street out of sight? She
swallowed nervously, and it hit me.

"Are you waiting for dope?" I said.

"You ain't no cop, are you?"

"No."

"Man's supposed to be here with some by
now."

"How often do you need it?"

"Two, three times a day."

"Get high?"

"Hell no. Just need it to feel okay, you
know, so's not to feel like shit. He tole me he
be here by now."

"He'll probably come soon. The white woman I was asking about. You talked to her, didn't you?"

"Why you think that?"

"Woman's intuition," I said.

The rain had begun. We moved as tight as we could against the wall. I smiled winsomely and held up the hundred. She took it and put it away, her eyes scanning the street as she did. On the corner a few yards away one of the other whores produced a big golf umbrella, which she must have stashed somewhere, and she and two other girls clustered under it. The umbrella was brightly striped in reds and yellows and greens. Like an odd flower in the gloom.

"She tell me she doing research," Jewell said. "She want to see what it was like on the street."

"Why did Jermaine let her talk with you?"

"Same reason he don't chase you off," Jewell said.

"Tony Marcus?"

"Un huh."

"She say why she's doing research?" I said.

"Say she work for some woman's company. Say they trying to find out about consent."

"Consent," I said.

"Un huh."

Jewell looked carefully at every man who passed on either side of the street. The other whores did likewise. They weren't looking for customers. They were waiting for Godot. The rain was steady. It was warm for the season, but cold for standing around in the rain. The building wasn't doing much of a job of protecting.

"Let's sit in my car," I said. "You can still see."

"Where's your car?"

"There, at the hydrant."

"Okay," she said. "You can get us some coffee in the drugstore first. Double cream, lotta sugar."

I said okay and went in and got us two large regular coffees. One with extra cream and four sugars. I came out and gave one to Jewell.

"Orlean," she shouted at the group of women under the umbrella. "I be sitting in her car, right there. He come, you holler for me."

Orlean said, "I will."

"You be sure you do, girl."

"I be sure."

We got in my car. I started it up, put the heater on low, turned the wipers on so Jewell would have a clear view of the corner.

"What kinda car is this?" Jewell said.

"Subaru."

"I ever get a car gonna be a convertible."

"I had one once," I said. "But your hair blows badly, and I have a dog, and I have to worry about her jumping out."

"I never had no dog," Jewell said.

"That's too bad," I said. "Tell me about this consent thing."

"She asking me about do I want to do this. I say sure. I don't want to do it, I wouldn't. And she say do I enjoy it? And I say what's to enjoy, giving some fat old guy with a limp dick a hand job in the front seat of his car? So she say that's so disgusting? Why do you do it?"

Jewell sipped some of her coffee and laughed.

"I say, don't you know 'bout money, sis? And she say but there are other ways to make money. And I say like what? Like being a doctor or shit?"

"And she say but there are other jobs."

"And I say not enough to support my habit."

Jewell drank some more coffee watching the street like a cat at a mouse hole.

"And she say maybe you can break that habit."

Jewell shook her head.

"That girl's been watching too much television," Jewell said.

"What do you suppose she had in mind?" I said.

"I axed her that. I say why you want to know all this crap 'bout consent and shit? She say she just gathering information."

Jewell finished her coffee, lowered the side window, threw the paper cup onto the sidewalk, and raised the window.

"That's all?" I said.

"There he is."

A young black man in baggy clothes with a Colorado Rockies baseball cap on backwards ambled up Mass Ave from the direction of the South End. Jewell was out of the car before I could say another word and walking toward the corner to wait for him.

The candy man can.

CHAPTER

35

JULIE'S FACE HAD a pinched look, as if it were cold in the Harvest, which it wasn't. I gave my coat to the hostess and joined Julie in the small bar to the right of the door.

"Hello," I said.

"Hello."

Julie was at a table for two. She had a glass of white wine in front of her. There was something sort of naked about her, like someone who always wore glasses and then didn't. When I sat down across from her, I saw that she wasn't wearing any rings.

I ordered a Coke.

"So how are you?" I said.

She shrugged, and twirled her wineglass.

"That good?" I said.

"I've left Michael," she said.

"Oh my."

She nodded.

"Yes," she said. "'Oh my'!"

"Where'd you go?" I said.

"I'm with Robert."

"If that doesn't work out," I said, "you're welcome with me and Rosie."

"Why wouldn't it work out?"

"Things don't always," I said.

Julie laughed without pleasure.

"I guess I should know that by now," she said.

"The kids with Michael?"

"Yes."

"Who looks after them during the day?"

"Same as before," Julie said. "Nanny."

"She a good mother?" I said.

"She's nice," Julie said.

"But?"

"But not smart."

"You have an arrangement to see them?"

"Informally."

"How are they?"

"They'll be fine."

"But now, are they not fine?"

"I haven't seen them since I left."

"What does Michael say?"

"I haven't talked with him."

"The nanny?"

Julie shook her head. She was starting to cry. Didn't I have the touch.

"I was drowning," Julie said. "I had to get out."

"Happens to a lot of women," I said.

"I just told the kids I was going away for a while."

"You need to tell them more," I said.

"I know it. Don't I know it? I'm a damn therapist, for crissake. Don't you think I know what I'm doing to my children?"

"A lot of marriages break up," I said. "A lot of children survive it."

"Little Michael is already a mess," Julie said. "What must he be feeling?"

"These are not moments when anyone feels good," I said, just to be saying something.

"I did what I was supposed to," Julie said. "I got married. I had children. I kept my career. I did everything I was supposed to."

I nodded. The waitress brought Julie another glass of wine. I hadn't seen her order it. Maybe it was a present keep-'em-coming arrangement she'd made before I got there. Julie drank some wine and looked at me.

"You didn't," she said.

"Do everything I was supposed to?"

"Yes."

"I'm still working on that," I said.

"Well so am I."

"Can I make one suggestion?"

"Of course."

"Don't do anything irrevocable right now."

"You think what I've done is revocable?"

"I don't know. I don't even know if it should be. But this is crazy time. This is the time to stay still and let things play out and see what you are feeling, and let that play out too."

"I know what I'm feeling."

"You know what you're feeling today."

"I can't go back," Julie said. "I'll die."

"You don't have to go back."

"Michael's so good. He loves his children. He works hard. He's home every night."

"But?"

"But I'm so bored. Kissing is boring. Sex is boring. Going out is boring. He has nothing to say. I prattle along. He listens. I don't think he cares. And somewhere underneath is disapproval. He wants more than I'm delivering. I know it. He lets me know it in ways I can't even explain."

"He know about Robert?" I said.

"No."

"Suspect?"

"I don't know. Sometimes I think he knows. Sometimes he seems oblivious."

"Probably both," I said.

"Well aren't you the clever little shrink," Julie said.

"I went through this, remember? I got some shrinkage in the process."

"Did you cheat on Richie?"

"No."

"But now you sleep around."

"I wouldn't say I sleep around. But if I'm dating someone, I expect to sleep with him. That's what grown-ups do."

"I never expected to be a woman who cheated on her husband," Julie said.

"I know," I said. "I never expected to be divorced."

"But you and Richie, you're sort of still together."

"We date," I said.

"Do you think you'll get back together?"

"I don't know. I'm pretty sure we won't get further apart."

"And you're happy?"

"Yes."

"God. I wish I were."

"Of course you're not now. Everything's too raw. But it doesn't mean you won't be. Just don't rush into anything."

"Like Robert."

"Just like Robert," I said.

CHAPTER

36

I WAS SITTING on the floor throwing the ball for Rosie. It was raining and she didn't like to go out in the rain, so I threw the ball the length of my loft and she dashed after it, and brought it back. A half hour or so of that was as good as a walk and kept her from getting so rambunctious that she broke things. I had my Lawrence B. Reeves file out and was looking at the calendar pad I had taken from his home. I rolled the ball down past my kitchen counter. Rosie tore after it. When she caught up with it, she nudged it with her nose to make it roll farther and when she finally trapped it against the baseboard at the far end of my loft, she picked it up and pranced back in an orgiastic frenzy of self-congratulation.

The calendar pad was marked as I remembered. "J" every Thursday night. Rosie dropped the ball and then snatched it back when I reached for it.

"Drop it," I said.

She dropped it and hunched over it like a

mother condor with her egg. I snatched it and threw it the length of the room again. She raced after it, all four feet clearing the floor, wrestled it into submission at the far end of the room and pranced back. In Lawrence B's phone book, under J, I found the listing: J, 254-2265. I reached my phone down from my bedside table near where I sat and called the number. It was a beeper. I punched in my home phone number and hung up. In maybe three minutes my phone rang. I picked it up and said hello.

"This is J," a voice said.

"J who?" I said.

The line went dead. It could have been Jermaine. Or it could have been Dr. J. Or J. R. Ewing. Or Jay Leno. I stood and shut off my answering machine in case J called back wondering who I was. I got my trench coat and put my gun in my belly pack. Then I put Rosie's leash on, which is a little like trying to lasso a hummingbird, and went down to get my car.

Rosie was asleep on the floor on the passenger side, with her nose stuck up near the heater vent, when I pulled in near the corner of Mass and Columbus and parked on the same hydrant I'd parked on before. I shut off the wipers so I wouldn't attract attention and waited, looking through the rain-blurred windshield, for Jermaine to make an appearance. It wasn't good weather for whoring. There were a couple of girls huddled against the wall of the drugstore, trying to stay dry. I thought they were probably more interested in the candy man than any johns that might be out in the rain.

Rain was a great beautifier. The worst streets looked as good as the best ones in the rain, when everything that could gleam did, and the neon lights looked like jewelry. I wondered why I thought of the whores as girls. I was as correct as the next person. But these were girls, not women. Many of them were very young, and probably qualified as girls. But even the ones old enough to be adults were still girls. It probably had something to do with dependence and independence.

I saw Jermaine's silver Mercedes pull up to the corner, the wipers disdainfully sweeping the rain off the windshield. Jermaine got out and left it running on the corner, compromising traffic. He had on a cowboy hat and a long yellow slicker. As he walked over to talk with the two girls by the drugstore wall, I called the pager number and punched in my car phone number. In a moment I saw Jermaine pause, open his slicker and look at his pager. He stared at it for a minute then took a cell phone out of his coat pocket and dialed. My car phone rang. I picked it up.

A voice said, "This is J."

I smiled and hung up. I saw Jermaine look at his cell phone for a moment. Then he dialed again. My car phone rang. I let it. After a while Jermaine punched off his cell phone and put the phone away. I sat for a moment staring at the way the rain moved across the surface of the windshield.

Lawrence B. Reeves had Jermaine Lister's phone number and some sort of standing arrangement with him on Thursday nights. Lawrence B. Reeves stalked Mary Lou Goddard and confessed to killing Gretchen Crane and killed himself—maybe. Gretchen Crane had come to Jermaine Lister to learn about prostitutes. Rosie looked like she needed to go out. I put her leash back on and got out of the car and walked up to the drugstore where Jewell stood with several other girls.

"Hey," Jewell said, "who that you got there?"

"That's Rosie," I said.

Jewell squatted down on her heels and put her face down to pat Rosie and let Rosie kiss her.

"You looking to give me more money?"

"You got something to sell?"

"Tell you 'bout the sister was with the honkie broad when she come to talk with me."

"Someone was with Gretchen?"

"Awful cold and wet out here," Jewell said.

"Want to sit in my car out of the rain?" I said.

"No. I like to stand out here and get soaked," Jewell said. "Saves taking a shower later."

"Want some coffee?"

"Yes."

"Extra cream," I said. "Lotta sugar."

I went into the drugstore. They didn't like having Rosie in there, but they didn't tell us to leave, so I bought two coffees and came back out. Jewell and I and Rosie got in my car. I turned it on and turned on the heater. I handed Jewell her coffee.

"You're like the postal service," I said.

"Huh?"

"Neither rain nor sleet nor snow nor dark of night...?"

"Jermaine likes us out every day."

Rosie got in the backseat but sat upright and stuck her head in between the front seats to make sure that nothing was consumed but coffee. Jewell patted her.

"When Gretchen, the white woman, came to talk with you about prostitution," I said, "who did she have with her?"

"Another woman," Jewell said. "A sister."

"A black woman?"

"Mostly," Jewell said.

"Why 'mostly'?" I said.

" 'Cause she black but she acting like some rich-bitch white broad," Jewell said. "She don't like talking with no whores."

"Was Gretchen that way too?"

"Yeah, but you know, you 'spect her to be."

"So what was the black woman's name?" I said.

"You mind if I smoke?" Jewell said.

"I hate it," I said.

"Well shit, honey, I got to smoke."

I pushed the window button and cracked the window on her side.

"Blow the smoke that way," I said.

She looked annoyed but she lit up and didn't say anything. She inhaled deeply and drank some coffee, and swallowed before she let the smoke out. She was restless and jittery. I realized the candy man was probably overdue again.

"The name," I said. "Did the black woman have a name?"

She didn't say anything. She was looking through the rain down Columbus Ave.

"Name?" I said.

"I'm thinking."

"Take your time," I said.

I didn't mean it. I knew if the candy man showed up I'd lose her.

"Worth something to you to know?" Jewell said.

I took my wallet out of my purse and opened it and took out the bills, and counted.

"I have twenty-eight-dollars," I said. "Unless you take MasterCard, that's how much it's worth to me."

"Honey," Jewell said.

"Honey what?"

"Don't know," Jewell said. "White broad called her Honey a couple of times. Just gimme the twenty. Don't want to take your last dollar."

I gave her two tens.

"You think maybe 'Honey' was just a term of endearment?"

"Huh?"

"Don't men sometimes call you Honey?"

"Oh, yeah."

"She never called her any other name?"

"Naw."

"What'd she look like?"

"Tall," Jewell said. "Taller than me. Good-looking. Hair real kinky, cut real short. Had some round glasses on with green, you know? What you call it? Not the glass part, but the...?"

"Frames," I said.

"Yeah, green frames."

"Anything else?"

"She a real white man's nigger, you know? Thin nose, thin lips, big eyes, got them cheekbones like the girls in magazines."

"You think they had a relationship?"

"Relationship? Like were they doing each other? That kind of relationship? Couple of dykes?"

"Yes."

"Maybe. White broad called her Honey."

"She call the white broad anything?" I said.

Jewell shook her head.

"She didn't?" I said. "Or you don't remember."

"Jesus, you ask enough fucking questions," Jewell said. "What difference it make?"

"I won't know what difference it makes until the end. It's why I'm careful."

"Well I tole you everything I know," Jewell said.

She shifted in her seat. Her coffee was gone. She was on her third cigarette.

"Why didn't you tell me this the first time we talked?"

"Don't pay to sell it all at once," Jewell said.

179

"If I come back with more money, is there more to tell?"

"I tell you stuff, long as you pay me," Jewell said.

She smiled widely.

"But from here on it'll be bullshit," she said.

"How about what you've told me."

"I like you. You got a nice dog and you don't act like you afraid you'll catch something talkin' to me," Jewell said.

"So what you've told me is true."

"Sho."

"But from now on you'll be lying for money?"

Jewell's smile got wider.

"Sho."

Rosie sniffed at Jewell's face for a moment and then began to lap it. Jewell giggled. Which Rosie took as encouragement and lapped more vigorously. Until Jewell put a hand up and pushed Rosie away gently.

"Well," I said. "I don't have any more money, so you don't have to lie. Doesn't that work out nicely?"

"Works out perfect," Jewell said.

We were quiet, Jewell gazing up Columbus Ave, waiting. It was, I realized, her life. Turning tricks to get money to buy heroin, waiting for the man with the heroin to show up and sell it to her. Turning more tricks to buy more heroin tomorrow. Or this evening. Or later in the day. Depending on how big a habit she had.

"You know a guy named Lawrence B. Reeves?" I said.

"What you think. The johns give me a calling card?"

"He came to you through Jermaine."

"Lotta johns do that," Jewell said.

"Middle-aged guy, maybe fifty. Pudgy, no style. He's bald in front and what's left he wears long and pulled back in a ponytail. Wears little round gold-rimmed glasses," I said. "Would normally be in action on Thursday nights."

"Larry," she said.

"Larry?"

"That's him. Jermaine bring him 'round every Thursday. One of us always takes him to the Bradley Hotel for an hour, haul his ashes."

"Anything you can tell me about him?"

"Got a really big dick," Jewell said.

"Really?" I said.

"Yeah. He don't look like he would," Jewell said. "But he do. All the girls want to do him so they get a look."

"Anything else about him?"

"Naw. They all weird."

"How is he weird?" I said.

"He like to pretend stuff, lot of them pretend stuff."

"What's he pretend?"

"He pretend I making him do this."

"What's he like afterwards?" I said.

"Just get up and leave. Don't say nothing," Jewell said. "This stuff turning you on?"

"No," I said. "I don't know why."

"Well he ain't much," Jewell said, "but he got a thing on him."

"Be still my heart."

CHAPTER

37

I WAS AT my kitchen counter with a yellow legal pad and a Bic pen trying to make a list. I loved lists. They made me feel organized. Unfortunately I barely knew enough about the death of Gretchen Crane to list anything. There were three black women employed by Great Strides. None of them was tall. None had a short haircut. And none wore eyeglasses with green frames. There had been no one, black or otherwise, hired or fired in the previous year. So "Honey" didn't come from the job. I looked up Natalie Goddard, who had taken Mary Lou's last name, in the phone book and found no listing. I called information and found it was non-pub.

Lawrence B. Reeves apparently used the services of Jermaine Lister, who had at least talked with Gretchen and her friend Honey. He had also stalked Mary Lou, and claimed posthumous credit for murdering Gretchen. Since everybody seemed connected to everybody else, a pattern should have been forming. It wasn't. The result of careful analysis produced the conclusion *so what?* While I was trying to figure out if *so what?* meant anything but *so what?* and finding that it appeared only to mean *so what?* my sister rang the bell and I buzzed her up. As soon as she came in the door, I knew that something had hit a fan somewhere. She was red-eyed and her face was haggard and she looked about twenty years older than I knew her to be. Rosie made a feeble attempt to wag and then forgot about it.

"So," I said, "how's your day?"

"I... I've broken up with Mort."

Although the reasons were nearly infinite, I felt it best not to say so.

"How come?" I said.

"He's a...a pig."

"Really?" I said.

"Yes. Don't pretend you didn't think so."

"Okay," I said.

"You could have warned me."

"No, I don't think at that point I could have. What particularly piggish thing did he do?"

She was staring at the floor between us. She shook her head.

"Okay," I said. "Would you care for coffee?"

Elizabeth scooched up onto a stool at my counter. She shook her head again. We were quiet. Down the loft where my easel stood the morning light was flooding it. The best time to paint. Or even to make a list. Not a very good time to be sitting silently with your unpleasant sister, while she stared at the floor and breathed deeply. To be doing something I made a notation on my list: *Mary Lou's girlfriend?* She was the only person I could think of connected to my murder case that I hadn't talked to.

"He wanted me and another woman," Elizabeth said so softly that I bent toward her to listen, "to have sex with him."

"Yuck," I said.

"You've never done that?" Elizabeth murmured.

"God no," I said.

"He said there was nothing wrong with it."

"There isn't, I guess, if it takes place among consenting, or maybe more accurately, willing, adults. I wouldn't be willing."

"Mort says I'm frigid."

"Mort's a reptile," I said. "It doesn't matter what he said."

"I did everything he wanted. I did sex things I'd never done before."

"Did you enjoy it?"

Elizabeth stopped looking at the floor and looked at me as if I had asked her to interpret the Bhagavad Gita. She didn't say anything as she thought about the question.

Finally she said, "I don't know. I was getting even with Hal."

I nodded and didn't say anything.

"He's furious at me for breaking up with him."

"Un huh."

"He has pictures of me."

"Of course he does," I said.

"He says if I don't come back to him, he'll put them on the Internet."

"A lot of adolescent boys will be pleased," I said.

"That's an awful thing to say."

"I meant it as a compliment," I said. Which was only partly true and I think we both knew it.

"What am I going to do?" Elizabeth said.

I knew there was that rivalrous ungenerous part of me that was enjoying the hell out of this. There's stuff you don't learn at Mount Holyoke. Stuff you have to ask your younger sister who didn't go to Mount Holyoke, and didn't marry an Ivy Leaguer. These were maybe the first two of the seven vices for Elizabeth. Though I was pleased to know that group sex was in the ranking.

"I don't know what to do," Elizabeth said. "What if Daddy sees the pictures?"

"He won't," I said. "He has no idea how the Internet works."

"But someone will tell him."

"It won't happen," I said. "I'll talk to Mort."

"By yourself?"

"No," I said, and smiled happily at the thought. "I'll bring Spike."

CHAPTER

38

SPIKE AND I found Mort Kraken's office in Waltham, in a warehouse filled with mismatched andirons, and frayed Chinese screens, and cracked toilets, and ceramic statuettes of shepherd girls, and paintings on velvet, and wrought-iron things, and a lot of knicks and a really large number of knacks. There were a couple of feral-looking helpers scuttling around the premises but no one paid us any attention.

"I wonder if he's in there battening on huge sea worms," Spike said.

"Doing what?" I said.

"It's a poem," Spike said.

"And a lovely one no doubt," I said and knocked on the office door, which had a pebbled-glass window with the word MANAGER in black paint across the middle of it.

"Yeah?"

"I'll take that to mean 'come in,' " I said to Spike and opened the door.

Mort was sitting at his desk without his rug, wearing a white shirt that looked as if it had been washed but not ironed. Over the shirt he had on a blue cable stitched cardigan sweater. He didn't look any better than he did the last time I saw him, but he was more suitable to his surroundings.

"Yeah?"

"We've met," I said. My name is Sunny Randall. I'm Elizabeth Randall's sister."

"Big deal," Mort said.

I looked at Spike and I could see the beginnings of a smile starting at the corners of his mouth. I closed the door behind us.

"You come to talk to me about dumping her, it's no use. She had her run, ya know. Now I'm moving on."

"Are you taking the nude pictures of her with you?"

Mort stared at me for a moment.

"I got no pictures," he said after a time.

"And therefore you won't be able to put them on the Internet," I said.

Then Mort made a bad mistake.

"Even if I did," he said, "they're mine. She wanted me to take them. You got no call telling me what to do with them."

Spike is not one of those chiseled gym rats. He is built like a bear. And like a bear he is both strong and very quick. He went around the desk, took hold of the back of Mort's shirt, yanked him out of the chair, and slammed him up against the wall, almost before Mort had stopped talking. Mort's feet were off the floor. He hit Spike, but Spike paid no attention.

"Why don't you step out, Sunny," Spike said, "and keep an eye out for the two desperadoes we saw on the way in."

"Help," Mort shouted.

Spike leaned close to Mort and whispered something in his ear.

Mort stopped struggling as if he'd been tranquilized. I stepped out into the warehouse and closed the office door behind me. The two scraggly employees were nowhere in sight. In about two minutes Spike opened the door and came out of Mort's office carrying a manila envelope. I looked past him. Mort was sitting quietly at his desk looking at nothing. Spike smiled and handed me the envelope.

"Nudies of Sis," he said.

CHAPTER

39

I BROUGHT ROSIE back from her morning walk and sat at the kitchen counter to have some coffee. Rosie did a variety of cute sits and looks in hopes of conning me into a second break-fast, but my trained detective's eye saw right through her ploy. I gave her a dog biscuit.

My list was still on the counter and was slightly longer than it had been. I needed to find out from Lee Farrell when Gretchen had died. I called him.

"Do we have a time of death on Gretchen Crane?" I said.

"The victim in the homicide we solved?"

"Yes," I said, "that Gretchen Crane. When did she die?"

"Oddly enough I still remember," Farrell said. "She was shot about eight hours before she was discovered."

"That would make it about midnight," I said.

"It's a pleasure to witness a trained investigative mind," Farrell said.

"In your job you probably don't get much

chance to do that," I said. "Do you have an address for Natalie Goddard?"

"Who the hell is Natalie Goddard?"

"Mary Lou Goddard's significant other."

"I didn't know she had a significant other."

"She lives on Revere Street, her number is non-pub."

"Hang on," Farrell said and I sat and listened to the faint hubbub of the squad room for a while, until Farrell came back on the phone and gave me the street number.

"Wow," I said. "It's a pleasure to witness a trained investigative mind."

Farrell hung up. I put the address on my list, and carefully noted the time of death too. It was not, for the moment anyway, illuminating. I didn't even know where I was on the midnight Gretchen died. Probably in bed, probably with Rosie. Still it is always better to have information than not to. I am more comfortable making a list when there's stuff written down. I had nothing else to do and nowhere else to go, so I gave Rosie another dog biscuit and a big kiss, and went to see Natalie. Revere Street is on Beacon Hill. One has more chance of bumping into Leonardo DiCaprio at the 7-Eleven than one has of finding a place to park in the Revere Street neighborhood. So I left my car at home and walked down and caught the subway and stared at my reflection in the glass and changed trains and got out at the Charles Street Station.

There's something Dickensian about Charles

Street. It is old and red brick, and scattered with shops. During the winter months you expect to see someone in a long muffler carrying home a fat goose. But on this raw spring day, no one was carrying anything to roast, though I saw at least one person hurrying along who looked sort of like a fat goose.

Natalie's address was a four-story town house halfway up Revere Street on the right-hand side. The front door had a peephole. There was no nameplate under the bell. I rang. In a moment I heard some movement behind the door. Then silence. Then the door opened six inches on a security chain and a woman looked out at me. I could only see a portion of her face, but it was the face of a black woman, and she was wearing eyeglasses with green frames.

Hot diggity!

I smiled warmly.

"My name is Sunny Randall," I said. "I got your name from Mary Lou Goddard. I'm looking into the death of Gretchen Crane, who, as you may know, was employed by Mary Lou at Great Strides."

She stared at me for a moment through her green-framed glasses. Then the door closed. The chain rattled and the door opened.

"Come in please."

I went into a small hallway with stairs rising along the left wall. To the right was an archway that opened into a living room. The town house appeared to be about one room wide, and since it was four stories high, if you lived here you'd have some pretty good quadriceps.

We went into the living room and sat. The front wall was mostly a bay window secured with safety mesh that unlocked from the inside. The walls were painted with English hunting scenes. There was an oriental rug on the floor whose tones were extended by the ceiling, which was painted maroon. The furniture was weighty, quiet, and expensive. I sat on the couch with my back to the front window and a coffee table in front of me. There were two copies of the *New Yorker* and a copy of *Entertainment Weekly*. Eclectic. Natalie sat across from me on a hassock, with her knees crossed and her hands folded over them. She was black. Her hair was cut very close to her head. She was tall, wearing faded blue jeans that fit her perfectly and an oversized white tee shirt that she hadn't tucked in and which hung to exactly the right length. Her running shoes were blue with yellow highlights and a lacing system that must have taken twenty minutes.

"Do you know who I am?" I said.

"You are the woman that was protecting Mary Lou from that dreadful stalker who killed poor Gretchen."

"Lawrence B. Reeves," I said.

"Yes. But I understood that case was solved."

She spoke like my sister Elizabeth, with a broad Seven Sisters accent.

"I'm just trying to clean up some loose ends," I said.

"I understood that Mary Lou had discharged you."

"Mary Lou refers to you as her significant other," I said. "Is that true?"

"We are lovers. I have even taken her name. Has Mary Lou discharged you?"

"What was your, ah, maiden name?"

"Mary Lou has discharged you," Natalie said. "I see no reason to speak with you further."

"Did you know Gretchen?" I said.

Natalie rose and walked to the hall and held the front door open.

"Good-bye, Ms. Randall."

I thought about asking her if she knew anyone named Jewell, or Jermaine. That might have gotten her attention, but I decided to keep what I knew to myself until I knew more. I got up and walked to the front door.

I said, "Thank you, Ms. Goddard." And left.

I decided to walk on up Charles Street and across the Common to the Park Street Station to catch the subway. It would allow me to think about what I'd learned.

Investigating is a funny business. After learning nearly nothing since the day I met Mary Lou, in one ten-minute visit I had learned that Natalie was almost certainly the woman with Gretchen when she'd talked with Jewell. That she wasn't eager to volunteer information. And that the magazines on her coffee table had little subscription labels that read Natalie Marcus.

CHAPTER

40

IT WAS BRIGHT and not quite as warm as the brightness would lead you to believe. I told Julie about Mort and Elizabeth as we walked together along the Charles in Cambridge, where Julie was now in residence. The Weld boathouse was behind us. And to our left, across Memorial Drive, the red brick dorms, which Harvard of course called houses, fronted the river.

"Do you think this Mort person will keep his word?" Julie said.

"Yes," I said. "I think Spike terrified him."

Julie smiled a little.

"Spike's unusual," she said.

"Yes," I said.

We crossed the Weeks footbridge and turned upstream with the river on our right now, with more red brick, this time the Harvard Business School on our left. There are several places in Cambridge where, in all directions except up, you could see only Harvard.

"Doesn't it bother you at all that sometimes you have to ask a man for help?" Julie said.

"No."

"But it makes you dependent."

"I think probably independence is a state of mind as much as a physical condition," I said. "I could shoot Mort, but I can't physically overpower him. Spike can. It's kinder to Mort to, ah, manhandle him, than shoot him."

"You could be in a business where you didn't need a man," Julie said.

"No," I said. "I couldn't. I need them to pick up things that are too heavy for me. I also need them for sex, for love, for both. Straight men need women in the same way. If I have children I'll need someone to sire them. I'd also like someone to father them."

"Do you want children?"

"I don't know. I try not to over-manage...besides, we have Rosie."

We crossed with the light at the Anderson Bridge and kept on along the river. Harvard Stadium was on our left. It was not red brick.

"Children should be so easy," Julie said.

"I know."

The eight-person crews, both men's and women's, were out on the river. The traffic was light on Soldiers Field Road and I could hear the voices of the crew coaches as we walked along.

"I..." Julie stopped and seemed to be rephrasing something.

"I can't live with anyone," she said.

"Really?" I said.

"Not even, God forgive me, my children."

"That must be painful."

"Painful? What can you know about painful? What kind of mother am I, I can't even stay and take care of my own children. What will happen to them? What must they be feeling?"

"They have their father," I said. "Michael's a good father, isn't he?"

"Yes. He's wonderful with them. It probably helps me feel inadequate."

"You'll see them, and when this works out, you can make it up to them. You're a good mother, Julie."

I wasn't convinced that I was right, but it seemed the thing to say at the moment, and friends are friends whether they're sane or not.

"I've gotten a little place of my own."

"And Robert?"

"We're still seeing each other, but he can't understand why I moved out on him too."

"How long have you been there?"

"Three days," Julie said

"How does it feel?"

"At night sometimes I get very scared, and think, 'What have I done?' But other times I feel as if I could just fly."

"I remember," I said.

"If everything else worked out, could you live with Richie?"

"Currently I don't," I said.

"Don't be so goddamned existential," Julie said. "I'm asking, could you?"

"I can sleep with him. I do that now. I could probably share a house with him...but it would need to be a big house," I said. "Does Michael know where you are?"

"No. I gave him my new phone number, and of course he knows where my office is."

"Have you talked?"

"By phone."

"How is that?"

Julie's face pinched and she dropped her head and didn't say anything. I knew she was trying not to cry.

"Time to get some help with this?" I said. "Besides me?"

Julie nodded. We reached the Eliot Bridge at the place where the river bends south. Julie stopped at the top of the arch and leaned on the bridge wall and stared down at the moving water. She nodded. I looked at the water with her.

"Will I feel better?" she said. "After a while?"

"Absolutely," I said. "I promise."

Her shoulders began to shake. I stood beside her and looked down at the water and tried to be a comforting presence while she cried.

CHAPTER

41

ON TUESDAY NIGHTS from 6 to 9 I had a composition class at B.U. I'd normally leave the house at 5:30 and get home about 9:20 and take Rosie for a walk. It was a valuable opportunity for Rosie to do her final day's business, and it was also important because she'd been alone in the loft for almost four hours and if she didn't get some exercise she would be picking up her ball and dropping it at my feet until I was ready to dive headfirst through one of the front windows.

The minute I came in the door, Rosie did a couple of spins and rushed to where her leash was hanging. She was so excited it was hard to get the leash attached but I did it and we dashed to the elevator and went down to the street. Five feet from the front door Rosie stopped suddenly and was motionless. She sniffed vigorously, her head raised a little, scanning back and forth with her nose. I looked around. There was nothing that I could see. The parked cars stood blank and silent at the curb.

"Come on," I said. "The danger seems to have passed."

Rosie looked at me and wagged her tail and set off ahead of me in that prancy walk she had. It was a bright evening, with a lot of stars, and the moon nearly full. We walked our usual route down to Fort Point Channel, and looked at the water, and turned and headed back. The pace was Rosie's. It was her walk, and I never dictated how long she could spend carefully snuffing an empty beer can. We always walked down on the near side of the street and back on the far side, so that Rosie could sniff her whole territory. It was nearly ten-thirty when we got back. As we crossed the street, Rosie's ears went back and she went into a crouch. Her little body elongated, her tail was out straight like a very short bird dog's. She was growling. We stopped. I had never seen her do this. She was very noisy when she saw another dog through the car window. But live, in the street, where the other dog might retaliate, she was normally as aggressive as a bunny. I looked around. Same empty street. Same blank cars parked in front of my loft. Rosie's low growl continued. She inched forward with her ears still flat and her belly almost touching the street. Since it was kind of showy to wear a gun in art class, it was in my purse. I took it out. Rosie's attention seemed directed at the entryway to my loft. In bad weather an occasional street person would take shelter there. But it was a warm clear night, and the entryway wasn't that comfy. I held the gun at my side and let Rosie lead me at a creep across the street toward the entry. As we reached the other side of the street, with the parked cars still between me and the doorway, I smelled cigarette smoke. I stopped. Rosie got even lower and her growl became more intense. I studied the doorway. Despite the moonlight it was still in deep shadow. Then I saw movement and the glimmer of something metallic. I went to my knees behind a parked car just before someone shot at me. There was a muzzle flash and the boom of a pretty big gun. And again, and a bullet ripped into the other side of the car I was behind, Rosie's aggressiveness had been dispelled by the gunfire and she was straining to run. There was a fog light on the front bumper of the car next to me, and I looped her leash handle over it. She scrabbled steadily to get away. I stayed still. The shooter couldn't stay in the doorway forever. People didn't, in fact, usually call the cops to report gunfire. But the shooter couldn't be sure they wouldn't and the strain would get to him. Sooner or later she would have to show herself...or himself. At the risk of sexism I thought the shooter was probably a man. He knew I was a woman and would be careless because of it. I squirmed behind the parked car to my left, and slid between a Honda and a Taurus. Behind me Rosie was still trying to run. She paid no attention to my move away. I felt bad for her. But I would feel worse if she was orphaned. I cocked my gun.

The shooter came out of the doorway. It was Jermaine. Good. He would be very scornful of a woman. And he was. He walked straight upright directly to the car where he thought I was. He had a revolver, which he was carrying casually at his side. Even now he was profiling. I slid between the Honda and the Taurus and and came up behind him and pressed the muzzle of my gun against the base of his skull, and grabbed a handful of his hair with my left hand.

"Move and I'll kill you," I said.

He stayed still.

"Drop the gun," I said. "Now."

He dropped it.

"Down on the ground," I said. "Flat on your face. Hands behind your head."

I gave him a little tap on the skull with the gun muzzle for emphasis. He did as I told him. When he was down I kicked his gun under one of the parked cars. Now that no one was shooting, Rosie was a bit calmer. She still strained at the leash but her feet were still. She wasn't spinning her wheels.

"Why are you shooting at me, Jermaine?"

"Fuck you, bitch."

"Not the right answer, Jermaine. I could shoot you in self-defense and no one would say a word."

"You can't shoot me in the back of the head and say it was defense."

"I could say you were trying to escape."

"You ain't got the balls."

"You try to get up and we'll see about the balls," I said.

I meant it. If he tried to get up I would shoot him. But he was right. I didn't think it was a matter of balls, exactly, but I couldn't shoot him in the back of the head while he lay on the sidewalk. I got my cell phone out of my purse and called the police.

Jermaine and Rosie and I must have been an odd tableau in the while that we waited for the cruiser in the moonlight. None of us had anything to say and we were silent for the entire time. One of the two uniforms that got out of the cruiser was a black woman named Emmy Jefferson I'd known at the Academy. The other cop was a white guy I didn't know. They both had their hands on their weapons. I kept my gun on Jermaine.

"Sunny Randall," she said. "Who you got?"

"Jermaine Lister," I said. "He attempted to kill me."

"You do that, Jermaine?" Emmy said.

The white cop handcuffed Jermaine. He was a big cop, with the kind of thick body that suggested a lot of time in the weight room. When the cuffs were on I let the hammer down on my gun and put it back in my purse and went over and picked up Rosie and held her in my arms. She was a quick healer. As soon as I picked her up, she started wagging and lapping. The white cop patted Jermaine down and then stood him up.

"His gun's under that car," I said. "There's one of his slugs in the car somewhere."

Emmy nodded.

"We let the crime-scene guys deal with that," she said.

She looked at Jermaine.

"I know you," Emmy said. "You run a string of whores."

"You don't know nothing," Jermaine said.

He wouldn't look at me.

"I know we going to put you away for a lot more than pimping, Jermaine," Emmy said. "Why'd you shoot at this lady?"

He wouldn't look at her either.

"Gun's under this Dodge," the white cop said. "There's a bullet hole in the door."

"Whyn't you put Jermaine in the car," Emmy said.

CHAPTER

42

ELIZABETH AND I were at her kitchen table. Rosie was in the car to ensure that she wouldn't shed a hair onto Elizabeth's carpet. The manila envelope that Spike had taken from Mort was lying between us, next to a sugar bowl and a cream pitcher on a small tray. They were decorated in a duck motif, and the spout on the cream pitcher was designed to look like a duck bill.

"You didn't tell Daddy, did you?" Elizabeth said.

How old would we be when she stopped competing with me for Daddy?

"No," I said. "I didn't."

"Did you look at the pictures?"

"Only enough to make sure it was you," I said. "Neither Spike nor I is interested in pictures of naked women."

"I guess I just don't understand about homosexuals," Elizabeth said.

"Probably not."

"What did Mort say?"

"Mort was in fear for his safety. I think he said, 'Help!' "

The Mister Coffee machine on the counter stopped gurgling and Elizabeth got us each a cup of coffee. The sugar bowl contained Equal. The duck-billed creamer contained skimmed milk. I stirred some of each into the coffee.

"You want to check the pictures," I said, "make sure they're all there?"

"Even if they are," Elizabeth said, "how do we know he doesn't have the negatives?"

"They're Polaroids," I said.

"What does that mean?"

"It means there are no negatives," I said. "Check the pictures."

"I don't wish to. They are embarrassing to me."

"Goddamn it," I said. "Check the pictures."

She took the envelope and went to the counter where I couldn't see, and took out the photographs. She looked at them quickly and counted them and put them back in the envelope.

"That's all the pictures I remember," she said.

"Do you want to burn them?" I said.

She was silent.

"Or not," I said. "I assume you haven't heard from Mort."

"No."

"How about Hal?"

"I haven't talked with him."

"Your lawyers talking?"

"I don't have a lawyer."

"Has his lawyer been in touch with you?" I said.

"I won't talk to him," she said.

"Hal or the lawyer?"

"Neither one."

"Have you told our father and mother any of this?" I said.

"Absolutely not."

"So just what is your plan?"

"I'm not going to let that sonofabitch divorce me so he can go live with his floozy."

"He can do that now," I said.

"If we can catch him, he won't be able to get his divorce. We can prove he abandoned me."

I drank some of the coffee. It would have benefited from cream and sugar. But Equal and skim wasn't so bad. Compared to Elizabeth most things weren't so bad.

"First of all," I said, "we have caught him. I don't plan to keep catching him over and over. Second, I don't know where you're getting your legal information. But I think you need a better source."

"You know the good-old-boy network," Elizabeth said. "All those damned lawyers are in cahoots."

"Get a female lawyer," I said.

Elizabeth looked a little puzzled, as if she had never thought of a female lawyer, and perhaps had never even thought that there were female lawyers. She couldn't seem to think that through, so she did what she always did.

"I don't need your help to run my life, Sunny."

"You need someone's help," I said. "This is too hard. You need a shrink. You need a lawyer."

"He'll find out he's made a mistake," Elizabeth said, "if he thinks he can walk out on me."

I nodded. We drank coffee in silence for a moment.

"Well, gotta run," I said.

"Of course," Elizabeth said.

We walked together to her front door, She seemed smaller to me than I always thought of her. It's probably why I didn't say, *You're welcome on the pictures.*

CHAPTER

43

LEE FARRELL CAME to see me. He was wearing a black suit with an Italian cut, a black shirt with a cutaway collar, and a black silk tie.

"Monochromatic," I said.

"Matches my gun," he said. "Jermaine claims he shot at you because you were messing with his girls."

"Mostly I was asking one of them questions."

"What's her name."

"I don't remember."

Farrell gave me a look. He was sitting in the wing chair my father usually sat in when he visited. Rosie was asleep on the floor with her head on his right foot.

"You don't?"

"Nope."

"That's funny," Farrell said. "I would have said you were someone would remember how many fillings she had."

"Six," I said.

"Un huh."

"Jermaine say anything else?" I said.

"Says he was just trying to scare you. He wasn't trying to shoot you."

"And you believe that?"

"Sure," Farrell said. "Would Jermaine lie?"

"Silly me," I said. "Of course not."

"How come you don't want to give up the whore's name," Farrell said.

"I don't think she's involved. If you question her, she'll get scared and never talk to me again."

"And?"

"And I kind of like her."

"Well, we can come back to her if we need to," Farrell said. "You have a theory?"

"Sure."

"Oh good," Farrell said.

"I think it's part of the whole thing with Gretchen Crane and Mary Lou Goddard and Lawrence B. Reeves."

"Those cases are closed," Farrell said.

"According to you. Not according to me."

"So, even if they weren't, what's it got to do with Jermaine?"

"I have 'messed' with one of Jermaine's girls, several times over the last several weeks. Why did Jermaine wait until now?"

"Procrastination?"

"I think I touched a nerve."

"Jermaine's nerve?"

"I don't know what nerve I touched yet. But I think there might be a Tony Marcus connection."

"That'd be fun," Farrell said. "Why do you think so?"

"Jermaine works for Tony," I said.

"Every pimp in the city works for Tony," Farrell said.

"Jermaine is sort of middle management," I said. "He's been auditioning to run the, ah, prostitution division, for Tony."

"You think Tony ordered the hit?" Farrell said.

"Maybe."

"Besides the fact that Jermaine is upwardly mobile," Farrell said, "you have anything else to make you think Tony sent him to shoot you?"

I tried to look enigmatic.

"Woman's intuition," I said.

Farrell looked down at Rosie, still sleeping on his foot.

" 'Woman's intuition,' " he said.

"I have some vague suspicions," I said, "about people who may be entirely innocent. Until I'm more sure than I am now, I don't want to let you guys trample on their flowers, so to speak."

"I wish I had woman's intuition," Farrell said.

"It's invaluable," I said. "Especially in crime fighting."

"So far we're getting nothing from Jermaine. If he's doing what Tony told him to do, we'll continue to get nothing."

"Because he's more afraid of Tony than he is of you," I said.

"Most people are," Farrell said. "Can you connect him?"

"If I do, it will be sort of a bonus," I said. "It's not exactly what I'm after."

"Which is?"

"What I'm after? I want to know who killed Gretchen Crane and why."

"You're not buying Lawrence B.?"

"I'm not buying Lawrence B."

"Well," Farrell said, "I can cut you some slack on this, I guess. You're Phil Randall's daughter. You used to be on the job."

"And you don't believe that Lawrence B. Reeves killed Gretchen Crane any more than I do," I said.

Farrell smiled at me. Then looked down at Rosie, who was still lying with her head on his foot.

"Excuse me," he said and bent over and gently moved her head, and stood up.

"I believe what I can prove," Farrell said.

"That's because you don't have woman's intuition," I said.

"I try to make do," Farrell said.

CHAPTER

44

RICHIE AND I tried to spend one weekend a month together. Since I live in a nearly door-less loft, lovemaking, with Rosie in residence, is awkward. If she's shut in the bathroom, she yowls. If she isn't, it becomes a ménage à trois. So when company is staying over, Rosie gets to visit Uncle Spike.

It was nine-thirty on a Rosie-less Sunday morning. Richie and I lay in my bed, with Richie's arm around me and my head on his chest and the sun coming through my skylight.

"That was nice," I said.

"Nice?"

"Sure," I said. "Nice."

"I suppose you think the Taj Mahal is nice."

"Yes. It's pretty nice."

We lay on top of the covers and were quiet for a while. With my head against his chest, I was aware of Richie's heart beating.

"Why was it again," Richie said, "that we got divorced?"

"Because you tended to idealize the marriage

so, that the reality was always disappointing you."

"Oh yeah, I knew there was a reason."

"We get along pretty well, now," I said.

"Yes."

"Are you happy the way we are now?"

"I'd be happier if we were monogamous."

"Day at a time," I said.

"Sure."

I always got a little claustrophobic when Richie talked about exclusivity. I didn't want to lose him, but I didn't want him all the time.

"It's not like I'm sleeping around," I said.

"You seeing anybody?"

"I love you, Richie, and I would die if you weren't in my life. But, at least for now, I can't let you become my life. I disappear too easily."

We were quiet again. Richie patted my shoulder. I rose up and kissed him on the mouth. When we were through kissing we looked at each other for a minute, at close range, and each of us smiled. "How's the case you're working on pro bono?" Richie said. "I heard somebody tried to shoot you the other night."

"How do you know that?"

"I know stuff," Richie said.

"And your family has police contacts," I said.

"Maybe a few," Richie said. "I hear that the shooter was a pimp named Jermaine Lister, and we think maybe Tony Marcus sent him."

"If he didn't, I don't know who did," I said. "Have I mentioned Natalie Goddard?"

"No."

213

"I talked to her on Thursday. She's Mary Lou Goddard's girlfriend. She took Mary Lou's last name."

"So?"

"So her name before she took Mary Lou's was Marcus."

"Small world," Richie said. "They related?"

"I don't know. But two people in the same case named Marcus?"

"It bears looking into," Richie said.

"That's my plan," I said.

"How are you going to go about it?" Richie said.

"I'm working on that."

"My father says you need some help, you should ask."

"Tell Desmond thank you," I said.

"He likes you. So does my Uncle Felix."

"And I like them," I said, "except that they're fucking criminals."

"Well...yeah," Richie said.

"I do like them. And I do appreciate the offer."

"Don't mess with Tony," Richie said. "He may not be tougher than you are, but he's meaner, and he's got more resources. If you go up against him, bring some people."

"Your father's people?" I said.

"They are experienced negotiators," Richie said. "Don't go up against Tony Marcus alone."

I nodded.

After a while I said, "It's good not to be alone."

"I know," Richie said.

CHAPTER

45

I TOOK ROSIE out for her morning ablutions. As I turned up Summer Street, a tan Toyota Camry pulled away from the curb in front of my house and inched along behind me. I stopped. It stopped. I stared through the windshield but the morning sun made the glass opaque. I looked around. There were several other dogs walking with people. Up ahead, a state cop in an orange traffic vest was steering cars past a set of construction barriers. It would take a hardy soul to clip me right now. As I stood and pondered it, the car pulled in by a hydrant, and the window went down on the passenger side. I walked over, and looked in.

"Buster," I said. "What the hell are you doing?"

"Felix told us to keep an eye on you."

Buster was a big man with very little neck and almost no hair on his head. He was one of the Burke family's troopers. The driver was slender with freckles and red hair, a blue tattoo showing on his right forearm where he had his sleeve half-rolled. I didn't know him.

"This here's Colley," Buster said.

"Hi, Colley."

Colley was looking straight ahead. He nodded without looking at me.

"Buster," I said. "I don't need an eye kept on me."

"Felix told us you'd say that."

"I don't want you following me around."

"Felix told us you'd say that too. But he says to follow you around anyway. He says Desmond don't want you hurt."

"Richie," I said.

"I don't know nothing about Richie," Buster said. "We work for Desmond and Felix."

I nodded. There was no point arguing. Buster wouldn't care what I said. He'd do what Felix Burke had told him to do.

"Is that a 'possum you got there?" Buster said.

"Rosie is a miniature bull terrier," I said.

"Sure," Buster said.

Beside him, Colley smiled, still staring up the street, his hands, one covering the other, resting on the top of the steering wheel.

"Well," I said, "I'm going to walk up there to the construction site. I'm going to walk back this way and leave Rosie in my loft. Then I'm going to come out and get in my car and drive over to Cambridge. I'm going to stop someplace and buy two cups of coffee and some bagels. Then I'm going to visit my friend Julie."

"Got that, Colley?"

Colley nodded.

Rosie and I finished our walk and I headed for Cambridge. Colley and Buster stayed behind me. Not so close that they'd have no time to react. Not so loose that I could lose them in the traffic. I took a couple of sudden turns just to see how they handled it. Colley handled it easily. I parked on Kirkland Street in front of a big old three-story mansard Victorian that had been chopped up into apartments. Julie's place was on the third floor. A kitchen, living room, bath, and bedroom. The place was furnished in early dorm: cheap maple-stained furniture, linoleum on the kitchen floor, a machine-braided red-and-green rug in the living room.

"I rented it furnished," Julie said. "Just until I could get organized."

"Looks fine to me," I said.

Julie closed the door behind me.

"I used to live in a mansion," she said.

By an absolute standard of mansion-ness, Julie was remembering her house with more nostalgia than accuracy. But compared to this place, she was right on the money. I took the coffee out and put it on her kitchen table.

"Got a plate?" I said.

Julie took a white plastic dinner plate out of the cupboard and put it down next to the coffee. I put three bagels on it.

"I don't have any cream cheese," Julie said.

"My thighs will thank you," I said. "Plain is fine."

We drank coffee and chewed bagel for a little while.

217

"So how's it feel living alone," I said.

"You should know," Julie said.

"I meant how do you feel living alone?"

Julie stared past me at the kitchen wall, on which someone had affixed flower decals. An Aunt Jemima notepad holder with no paper in it hung beside the wall phone.

"Scared."

"Everyone is scared at first."

"You too?"

"Sure, you wake up at night thinking *My god what have I done? Where's my house, my husband, my life?*"

"Where are my children?" Julie said.

I nodded.

"At least you got the dog," Julie said.

I nodded again.

"Do you want to go back?" I said.

"I can't."

"You don't have to."

"Does the fear pass?"

"Absolutely," I said.

"God I don't know what to do."

"You've done something already," I said. "You don't have to do something else right away."

Julie nodded. She was barefooted, wearing jeans and a black tee shirt. Her hair was done, but she wore no makeup.

"I need to borrow your brain for a bit, if I may."

"I don't know how much use it will be to you right now," Julie said.

"Let me give you the outline of a case," I said.

She nodded.

"Mary Lou Goddard asked me to protect her from a stalker named Lawrence B. Reeves. I agreed. Then a woman named Gretchen Crane, who worked for Mary Lou and somewhat resembled her, was murdered. Then Lawrence B. Reeves was found shot dead. There was a suicide note saying he killed Gretchen mistaking her for Mary Lou. The cops liked it. It cleaned up two murders for them. But I didn't believe it. So I kept on. I found out that Mary Lou in fact had a sexual relationship with Lawrence B. even though she is aggressively lesbian. That she has a girlfriend, a black woman, Natalie Goddard. They were so committed a couple that Natalie took Mary Lou's last name, though they don't live together."

"A lot of that going around," Julie said.

She had broken one small segment off of her bagel and was eating a small bite of that.

"I also discovered that Gretchen was investigating prostitution with the thought of rescuing whores from a life of depravity, and maybe organizing them politically."

Julie snorted. I shrugged.

"In this quest she came into contact with Tony Marcus, who runs prostitution in this part of the world. He sent her to a pimp named Jermaine Lister. Jermaine let her talk with some of his whores, and when she did that she was often accompanied by Natalie, who was apparently helping her with this project."

"Natalie was Mary Lou's girlfriend," Julie said.

"Right."

"Was she having an affair with Gretchen?" Julie asked.

"I would guess so," I said. "Plus, her name before she look the name Goddard was Natalie Marcus."

"The same as Tony, the gangster."

"Exactly."

"Is he black too?"

"Sure."

"Do you think Natalie is related to Tony?"

"After I talked with her, Jermaine..."

"Now who's Jermaine?"

"The pimp that Tony sent me to. Jermaine tried to kill me."

"My God."

"It's okay," I said. "He didn't. The cops have him now, and are trying very hard to turn him. They would love to get Tony Marcus."

"Can they?"

"He claims that he did it on his own because I was bothering his girls."

"And you think?"

"He did it because I was talking to Natalie Goddard/Marcus and there's a connection that Tony doesn't want known. But I think Jermaine's too afraid of Tony to ever implicate him."

"Well that's certainly complicated," Julie said.

"It's worse, or better, depending how you think about it. Lawrence B. Reeves, the lover/stalker of Mary Lou Goddard, used to have a regular weekly appointment with a hooker named Jewell, who was one of Jermaine's girls."

"What a tangled web we weave," Julie said.

She finished her coffee, looked into my cup to see that I had finished mine, then picked up both cups and got up and put them into a white plastic wastebasket. She leaned her hips against the kitchen counter and folded her arms.

"I haven't talked to my kids," she said. "Michael won't let me."

I nodded.

"In a way I don't blame him. He's very angry with me. But I have the right to talk with my children, don't I?"

I stood and walked to the window and looked down at the street. I could see Buster and Colley double-parked beside my car. I had to admit it was sort of comforting. I turned back to Julie.

"Of course you have a right to talk with your children," I said. "You don't need me to tell you that."

"I'm just so fragmented," Julie said.

"Goddamn it," I said. "I have listened, commiserated, counseled, advised, and cared about everything you said since the shit first hit the fan. Now I'm asking you to listen to me for a minute. It might even be good for you to stop thinking about yourself, however briefly."

Julie stared at me. Her eyes began to fill with tears.

"Come on, babe," I said. "Muscle up. I need your help."

She was silent, looking at me. Then she turned and bent over the sink and splashed cold water on her face. She wiped it dry with a paper towel. Put the towel in the trash and sat back down at the table.

"You're right," she said. "Let's you and me think through this Mary Lou thing."

Which we did.

Three hours later the sun had shifted west enough to come slanting in through the ugly little back window in Julie's ugly little kitchen. Buster and Colley were still parked outside. And Julie had a couple of pages of yellow notepaper filled with notes and scribbles, and relationship trees, and arrows pointing to various names.

"What are we looking for?" she said.

"Pattern," I said.

Julie laughed slightly and without amusement.

"That may be too big a demand to place on life," she said.

"Just because your life is confused," I said, "it doesn't mean all life is confused."

"No? You think I'm projecting?"

"Isn't it sort of self-dramatizing, to assume that your angst is universal?" I said.

Julie smiled at me.

"Damn," she said. "You're thoughtful for a girl detective."

"Maybe it's why I'm a detective," I said.

Julie widened her eyes at me and went back to looking at her notes.

"Well," she said, "there's a little pattern."

"Sexual deceit?" I said.

"That's part of it, but there's an even larger pattern."

"Tell me about the pattern," I said.

"Why bother if you see it too?"

"You helped me see it, maybe you'll help me understand it."

"Well!" Julie said. "Thank you."

"You're welcome," I said. "You're pretty thoughtful for a girl therapist."

Julie laughed. The laugh sounded real.

"Maybe it's why I'm a therapist," she said.

"What do you see?"

"Offbeat sex. Illicit sex. I don't know what the right word is, inappropriate sex."

"Ah yes," I said. "The therapist's word for weird."

"Inappropriate? Yes. It's a useful word. For instance Mary Lou cheated on Natalie with Lawrence," Julie said. "That would be inappropriate."

As she talked her whole persona became professional. She was no longer the confused and frantic adolescent. She was being her adult self.

"Natalie maybe cheated on Mary Lou with Gretchen. Lawrence, I don't suppose you'd call it cheating, they probably didn't have much of a relationship, but you wouldn't call it fidelity either, made regular visits to Jermaine's whores while he was apparently wooing-slash-stalking Mary Lou. Jermaine, who tried to shoot you, sold sex for Tony Marcus, who might be related to Natalie, who was with Gretchen when she talked to Jermaine and to—what was her name?—Jewell, who was some of the sex which Jermaine sold. Whatever else it's about, this case is about sex."

"Suppose it is," I said. "Where do I start to look?"

Julie tapped her lips with her fingertips gently for a moment.

"Do you know the Robert Frost poem 'Fire and Ice'?"

"Detectives don't read poetry," I said.

Julie nodded.

"Therapists do," she said and put her head back and looked up toward the ceiling and narrowed her eyes and recited the poem, adding emphatic intonation to the last lines...

> *"I think I know enough of hate*
> *To say that for destruction ice*
> *Is also great*
> *And would suffice. "*

"Revenge?" I said.

"With all that sex, covert and open, there's got to be some jealousy someplace," she said. "I'd start with the Natalie–Mary Lou relationship."

"Same passion," I said. "Different application."

Julie smiled. It was the slightly superior smile of a therapist talking to an amateur, but it was a genuine smile, which was something I hadn't seen much from her lately.

"Something like that," she said.

46

I WAS AT my easel, the next morning, under the skylight catching the best light of the day, when Lee Farrell called me.

"Jermaine got shanked in the jail yard," he said.

"Dead?"

"Yes."

"Do you know who did it?"

"I don't know who put the knife into him," Farrell said.

"But you assume Tony Marcus had it done."

"That's what I assume," Farrell said.

"To make sure he didn't tell anyone about Tony sending him to shoot me."

"That's what I assume."

"Which, if true, would mean that it was Tony, and then the question would be *why?*"

"Except," Farrell said, "we don't have a rat turd of evidence that Tony had anything to do with it."

"So you haven't asked him," I said.

"No. You have any thoughts?"

"Well, Jermaine must have known something that Tony didn't want him to speak of."

"Wow, you are Phil Randall's kid."

"No need for sarcasm," I said. "Just because I stated the obvious doesn't mean it isn't obvious. The question is, what did Jermaine know?"

"Maybe Tony had him zipped because he was supposed to kill you and failed," Farrell said. "Sort of a long-term demotion for incompetence."

"Maybe, but even so, why did he want me killed?"

"Tony's got a secret," Farrell said.

"Either way," I said.

"You have a guess," Farrell said.

"It's connected to the Gretchen Crane murder," I said.

"Isn't everything."

"You remember Mary Lou Goddard," I said.

"Un huh."

"She has a girlfriend who took her last name, Natalie Goddard."

"Yeah?"

"Natalie Goddard's former name was Natalie Marcus."

"Honest to God?"

"Honest to God."

"Hold on a minute," Farrell said.

He went off the line for a moment, and I could hear some rustling of paper in the background before he came back on.

"There is half a column of people named Marcus in the Boston white pages," he said.

"Maybe it's just a coincidence," I said.

"And a weak one. Even if she is related. It doesn't say anything about who killed Jermaine Lister."

"That's why I didn't mention it before."

"I was going to get to that," Farrell said.

"You had the case closed on Gretchen Crane," I said.

"Still is," Farrell said. "But now we have the Jermaine Lister case and that's open."

"And now I told you," I said.

Farrell was quiet for a minute on the phone.

"I hate coincidences," he said. "They don't get you anywhere."

"True," I said.

"How old is this woman?"

"Maybe forty," I said.

"Too old to be Tony's daughter. Could be a wife or sister. I'll check a little."

"And let me know what you find out?"

"It's my reason for living," Farrell said.

CHAPTER

47

I HAD JUST fed Rosie her breakfast when I got a call from my sister.

"I got some legal papers in the mail," she said.

"Hello," I said.

"I need you to go over them with me."

"Who they from?"

"Hal's lawyer. They came registered mail or whatever it's called and I signed for them before I knew what they were. Can you come over."

"No."

"No?"

"No."

Rosie was vigorous and forthright in her dining habits. She was eating her dog food quickly, making a steady crunch noise as I talked.

"Sunny, you're my sister," Elizabeth said after a while. "I need your help."

"I don't go over legal papers with someone. Lawyers do that. You need a lawyer."

"Did you have a lawyer?"

"Yes," I said. "The divorce was amicable, but you have to have a lawyer."

"Was he any good?"

"She was just right," I said. "But she won't do you any good. She's a judge now."

"A woman judge?"

"I can get some suggestions from her."

"I wouldn't want a woman," Elizabeth said.

"What about the old-boy network?"

"I would want a male lawyer."

"Okay, I'll get you some names."

"Find out where they went to school," Elizabeth said.

"School?"

Rosie had finished her breakfast and was nosing the dish around the kitchen area in case there was a stray kibble.

"Certainly. I have to be able to judge," Elizabeth said. "I mean I don't want some lawyer who graduated from the University of Pittsburgh or something."

Rosie gave up on the stray kibble and turned to her water dish. She drank loudly.

"On second thought," I said, "you better find your own lawyer."

"Me?"

"Yes."

"Alone?"

"Um hm."

"I don't know anything about lawyers."

"You were married to one for seventeen years," I said.

"Sunny, you have to help me," Elizabeth said.

"I am helping you," I said. "I'm helping you grow up."

"Grow up, for God's sake, I'm three years older than you are."

"Chronologically," I said.

"What?"

"Never mind. It's time you learned to be on your own, to recognize what kind of help you need, and figure out how to get it."

"What the hell are you talking about," Elizabeth said.

I could hear her voice making up its mind whether to cry.

I tried a different approach. "The best revenge is living well," I said.

"Honestly," Elizabeth said, "half of the time I can't follow you at all."

"Well maybe if you showed him you don't need him, that you can function fine on your own, he'd be sorry."

I didn't believe a word of it. But I was trying all avenues.

"Goddamn him," she said.

"Hal?"

"Of course, Hal. If he hadn't left me I wouldn't be in this terrible situation."

"He didn't leave you," I said. "As I recall, he cheated on you. You caught him, and kicked him out."

"You're the one who caught him," Elizabeth said.

"Goddamn me?"

"Daddy will help me," Elizabeth said. "He'll understand."

"As, I'm sure, will our mother," I said.

It was unkind. No one could elicit unkindness like Elizabeth.

"Oh God!" she said.

Her voice made up its mind. She started to cry. I listened for a while. Finally she paused to breathe.

"It's your chance," I said, "to get rid of all the nonsense that clatters around in your head. It's your chance to grow up, to discover that you're enough."

"What?"

"You need courage, intelligence, a shrink, and a lawyer. No one can acquire any of them for you. You are on your goddamned own here, and I do you no favors if I let you think you're not."

She sniffled a little.

"You still see Richie," she said.

"Richie and I have a relationship that works for us. It is possible only because we don't need each other to be complete. You understand that?"

"You can talk, you've had a bunch of jobs."

"I can talk because I'm right."

"I've never even had a job," Elizabeth said.

"Probably time that you got one," I said.

"Sunny," she said with the sniffles still trembling in her voice, "what have I done to make you so angry?"

I took the phone away from my ear and held it and looked at it for a moment and realized I had nothing else to say and put the phone gently back in its cradle.

CHAPTER

48

BECAUSE I WAS going to be gone for a while, I gave Rosie a big soup bone to work on. She dashed with it over to my bed and jumped up. This meant that when I came home there'd be soup bone juice all over my spread, but the spread was washable, and even if it weren't, Rosie liked it there.

I drove over to the Back Bay and found a parking space on Clarendon Street near Commonwealth, on my fourth time around the block. I ignored the meter. It would run out before I came back and I'd get a ticket anyway. The day was lovely. Temperature in the seventies, sun in the sky. No wind. I waved at Buster and Colley idling in their tan Camry near where I'd parked. They followed me as I walked down Commonwealth and cut across the public garden and headed down Charles to Revere Street. Charles was one-way, the other way, and the Camry couldn't follow me, so Buster got out and followed me on foot until Colley circled the block and met me as he came up Charles Street. Buster got back in and they parked illegally near the foot of Revere Street where they could see me, as I took up my post, as inconspicuously as I could, outside Natalie's apartment.

I had on a big hat and a summer dress and my gun in my shoulder bag and big sunglasses, Oakleys, the kind that wrap around. Sunny Randall, mistress of disguise. I had a choice of Natalie or Mary Lou. And took Natalie. I needed a picture of her. And I was also working on the premise that she was easier to get to and more likely to go somewhere that I could follow. As far as I knew she didn't work.

I hadn't thought about that before. But now it suddenly registered. Did Mary Lou support her? Was she wealthy? Did she have an ex-husband paying alimony? I had ample time to think about it because no one came or went in Natalie's apartment all morning. In fact I had time to think about that, about Elizabeth, about Julie, about Richie and me, about a detective named Brian whom I'd liked very much but not enough to love him, and not quite enough to give up Richie for him, about how Rosie managed to be so expressive with so immobile a set of features, about how magically Vermeer got that quality of bright light into his paintings...and then about how elegant Natalie looked as she came out her front door wearing a long cream-colored coat over a short cream-colored skirt. She paused on the top step, letting the outdoors soak in for a moment.

I followed Natalie down Charles Street and across the Public Garden. The swan boats had made their spring debut, and cruised tourists and their children serenely around the small lagoon. Natalie crossed Arlington near the George Washington statue and went in the front door of the Ritz. It was lunchtime, so I lingered briefly outside, and then went around to Newbury Street and checked through the windows into the café. Natalie was there, across the table from Mary Lou.

I loitered near the window, gawking at Newbury Street and sneaking a frequent peek at the two women. The waiter brought each of them a glass of white wine. As they sipped the wine and looked at their menus, I formulated a plan. It was one of my favorite parts of detective work. Especially if the formulation worked.

I went into the café just after they gave the waiter their lunch order. I told the maître d' I was joining them and walked to the table.

"Well," I said, "what a pleasure."

Natalie didn't speak.

Mary Lou said, "What do you want?"

"Just a couple of questions while I've got you both together."

"We have nothing to say to you. Please go away."

I leaned over the table toward Mary Lou and knocked Natalie's wineglass over with my left hand.

"Oh my God," I said. "I'm so terribly sorry."

I snatched the wineglass up and began to dab at the spilled area with a napkin. The waiter rushed over with more napkins.

"Let me buy you a new glass," I said. "And if there's any on your suit…"

Instead of being grateful that it wasn't red wine, Natalie seemed concerned that some had gotten on her suit and was rubbing at it frantically with a napkin dipped in water. Mary Lou stood up.

"Never mind that. Just go away. Goddamit, just get the hell away from us."

I knew where I wasn't wanted. I put Natalie's glass in my bag and went away, while the waiter and Mary Lou and Natalie and the maître d' hovered around the spilled wine. Outside, on Newbury, Colley and Buster were double-parked in the tan Camry. I walked over to the car, opened the back door, and got in.

"Give me a ride to my car, please."

"What the hell was that all about?" Buster said.

"Fingerprints," I said.

CHAPTER

49

I WAS ALREADY at the bar at a place on Columbus Avenue called Club Café when Lee Farrell came in and sat down beside me.

"Sorry I'm late," he said. "Half the city is dug up."

"And expensively so," I said.

"I just live down the street here," Lee said. "In the South End. Used to be able to walk to work until they moved headquarters."

"Nothing stays the same," I said.

Farrell had a Beefeater martini straight up with olives. I was having a Kettle One gimlet made with fresh lime juice. Farrell raised the martini so that he could look at it against the light behind the bar. Then he gestured with it at me, and we clinked glasses.

"We got four sets of prints off the wineglass," Farrell said. "Yours. Another set we got no record of. Probably the bartender's. A set belonging to a guy named Solomon Cruz, got busted in 1988 on a numbers charge. Nothing more recent. Probably the waiter. And a pair belonging to Verna Lee Lister, who got arrested about a dozen times before 1995 for soliciting."

"Lister?"

"Uh huh."

"Like Jermaine?"

"Un huh."

"Christ," I said. "Is she related to everybody?"

"Maybe."

"And she was a hooker?"

"If those were her prints," Farrell said.

"Jesus Christ," I said.

"You think her partner knows?"

"I don't know what anybody knows," I said. "Every time I look into anything to do with this whole case, it turns out that things are not what they seem and people are lying about it."

"Lot of people lie about a lot of things," Farrell said. He took a sip of his martini. "World's dishonest."

"Well, aren't you the philosophical one," I said.

"Being a cop you don't usually get to direct your feet to the sunny side of the street."

"I recall."

"Still, there is some valid reason to wonder whether Lawrence B. did the murder. So if he didn't do it," Farrell said, "who did?"

"It's the closest you've come to admitting you don't think he did it," I said.

Farrell shrugged. "The question stands," he said.

"I know. I wish it didn't."

"You have a theory?"

"All I'm working on now is that there was something wrong with the relationship between Natalie and Mary Lou."

"That's your theory?"

"Yep."

"Isn't that swell," he said.

I shrugged.

Farrell sipped more martini and let it settle with obvious pleasure. "When I came in," he said, "I noticed a couple of hard cases hanging around outside in a tan Camry."

"They're from Richie's father," I said. "He and Richie's uncle heard someone tried to shoot me and they sent bodyguards."

Farrell smiled.

"Thoughtful in-laws," Farrell said.

"Ex-in-laws."

"I hear you're still seeing Richie."

"I see him. I'm not married to him."

"A girl needs her space," Farrell said.

"Or something," I said.

"You think Richie put them up to it?"

"He says he didn't."

"You believe him?"

"Yes."

"You want me to chase the bodyguards off?"

"No. They'd just come back. You know the Burkes."

"Yep."

"And to tell you the truth, they make me feel more secure."

"They would me," Farrell said.

239

CHAPTER

50

I WENT OVER to the new headquarters the next day and looked at mug shots of Verna Lee Lister.

"Yes," I said to Farrell. "She looks a lot different now, but it's Natalie."

"Good," Farrell said. "I thought I might run at this from the other end, so I went over to the Organized Crime Unit this morning before you came, and looked at Tony Marcus in their computer."

We were sitting at Farrell's desk in the squad room. It was neat and efficient-looking like the whole building, still new. Cynicism and sorrow had not soaked into its walls yet. The paint was still fresh.

"That's very thoughtful of you," I said.

"OCU busted him in 1997 for Criminal Conspiracy."

"I gather they didn't make it stick."

"Naw. They knew they couldn't. They just like to hassle Tony whenever they can. He made bail in a couple of hours, and the case got dismissed in the prelim."

He opened a manila folder and took out a computer printout and handed it to me.

"Take a look at who put up bail."

"Natalie Marcus, spouse."

"There," Farrell said. "Now go solve your case."

"Solve?" I said.

"Sure, I've done all the heavy digging for you."

"You bet," I said. "The walk to OCU must have been exhausting."

"Hey, I got you the identity of your black woman. I established she was married to Tony Marcus."

"I know," I said. "Thank you. It's just that the more information I have, the more I can't figure it out."

"If I'm investigating a murder," Farrell said, "which I'm not, because this case is closed, and Tony is in the mix, I'd figure him for a hand in it."

"Maybe if I start with him," I said.

"And work backwards," Farrell said.

"I wonder if he's still married to Natalie."

"Be worth finding out, I guess."

"That's pretty much what it all is, isn't it," I said. "You find a question and you try to answer it. And when you get enough answers, something begins to form."

"Or it doesn't," Farrell said.

"I know. We both know you don't always solve the crime."

"Hell, Sunny, you were on the job. You know that sometimes we're not even trying to solve the crime. We're just trying to clear the case."

"I know," I said. "That's my advantage. I only have to worry about solving the crime, and I can work on it as long as I want to."

"Or until you go broke."

"Usually I have a client."

"And in this case?"

"I might sell a painting."

"Un huh."

I smiled at him.

"And my ex-husband has money."

"Alimony?"

"Oh God, no," I said. "I'd never ask Richie for alimony."

Farrell nodded.

"Of course not," he said.

"Alimony destroys a relationship."

"I figured the divorce usually did that."

"It doesn't have to, and even if it did, alimony destroys women. It leaves a woman still dependent on the man she divorced."

"How about she's raising the kids," Farrell said.

"Parents should support their children," I said.

Farrell nodded.

"You start investigating Tony Marcus," he said, "you should do so very carefully."

"Maybe he needs to be careful of me," I said.

"You don't have to prove you're tough, Sunny. We all know you are. But Tony would have you shot for stepping on his shadow if he were feeling grumpy that day. He already sent one guy after you."

"I wonder why it was Jermaine," I said. "I wonder why it wasn't Ty-Bop."

"That's a pretty good question," Farrell said. "For a girl."

"You hadn't thought of it either, had you?"

"Maybe I did," Farrell said. "Maybe I didn't."

"And maybe you're a horse's ass," I said.

"I didn't know that was still in doubt," Farrell said. "But why didn't he send Ty-Bop?"

"Maybe he didn't send Jermaine."

"Then why in hell did Jermaine try to shoot your ass?"

"Good question," I said. "For a boy. Maybe it has to do with the same last name."

"Just be glad he didn't send Ty-Bop."

"Ty-Bop's a skinny adolescent hop-head," I said.

"Yeah," Farrell said, "with the life expectancy of a fruit fly. But he can shoot. And he likes to shoot. And he would shoot everyone all the time if Tony didn't control him. If it had been Ty-Bop you wouldn't be here."

"Glad it was Jermaine," I said.

CHAPTER

51

WHEN NATALIE CAME down the steps of her house, wearing designer sweats and running shoes, I fell in beside her.

"I do not wish to talk with you," Natalie said.

"No. I don't blame you," I said. "But you may as well get it over with now. You know how persistent I am."

Natalie kept moving, down Revere Street toward the river. I stayed with her.

"I know nothing about you," Natalie said, "except that you are an intrusive bitch."

"I don't think feminists are supposed to say 'bitch.'"

"You'd be quite surprised at what I can say." Natalie picked up her pace a little.

We walked in silence to the footbridge near the Arlington Street exit from Storrow Drive, and up over it, and down onto the esplanade near the Hatch Shell. Natalie tried to outwalk me, but I stayed with her.

"What do you want?" Natalie said. If her voice weren't so high-toned and well bred, she would have snarled.

"What is your relation to Tony Marcus?" I said.

Natalie's head snapped around as if it were electrified.

"Get away from me," she said with her teeth clenched.

"When did you stop turning tricks?" I said.

She stopped. I stopped with her.

"You lousy little fucking honkie bitch," she said with her teeth clenched even tighter. "Get the fuck away from me or I will kick your nasty little blond ass."

So much for well bred.

"Does Mary Lou know about your past?" I said.

She kicked me. She was off target from her threat and got me in the knee. She started swinging at me with both hands. She didn't show a lot of skill, but she was enthusiastic and several punches landed before I was able to get a hold of her right arm. I ducked under, and twisted her arm up behind her and held it with my right hand while I got hold of her hair with my left hand.

"I'm slender," I said, "but I'm quick."

Natalie struggled but there wasn't a lot to struggle against.

"I can do this longer than you can," I said. "Why don't you quiet down."

"Fuck you, bitch."

"Calm down," I said. "Or I'll dislocate your shoulder."

"Motherfucker!"

I gave her arm a small twist.

She said "Ow!" and stood still.

"Better," I said.

"Your former name is Natalie Marcus," I said. "You paid Tony Marcus's bail in 1997 and were listed on that occasion as his spouse. You were formerly known as Verna Lee Lister and you were arrested numerous times prior to 1995 for soliciting."

"So?"

"What makes it more interesting is that a pimp named Jermaine Lister tried to kill me a little while ago, and got arrested for it, and was stabbed to death in the jail yard."

"Jermaine?"

"Yep. There's a lot of name coincidence here, isn't there?"

"Somebody killed Jermaine?"

"Did you know Jermaine?"

Natalie began to cry. Not loudly, more stifled and interior. I let her go and she went and sat on a bench near the water. I sat beside her.

"You did know Jermaine."

She nodded.

"Husband?"

She shook her head.

"Brother," I said.

She nodded.

"I'm sorry," I said.

Natalie didn't speak. She stared at the water and cried.

"Do you know who had him killed?" I said.

Natalie continued to stare at the river as it moved slowly east toward the harbor.

"Do you know who killed Gretchen Crane?"

Stare.

"Do you know who killed Lawrence B. Reeves?"

Stare.

"Natalie," I said, "I know who all the players are. I know most of the connections. It's only a matter of time before I dig it all up."

While she stared, Natalie began to take deep shaky breaths. I waited. She didn't speak or look at me. One had to be tougher than I am to keep pushing her. I stood.

"I'm sorry about your brother," I said. "And I'm sorry you had to learn it this way."

She kept looking at the river and crying and breathing hard. I left.

CHAPTER

52

I SAT WITH Mary Lou Goddard in her office at Great Strides. She was nowhere near as friendly as Natalie had been.

"Almost from the day I met you and that disgusting little dog," Mary Lou said, "I have regretted it."

The insult to Rosie seemed gratuitous, but since Rosie wasn't there to hear it, I let it go.

"You might regret it more," I said.

"You are too insignificant for me to regret it more. You are an intrusive, nosy, self-serving woman who has no sense of her place in the larger order of things."

"The larger order of things?"

"We have serious work to do here. You seem intent on impeding it."

"That may be a collateral effect," I said. "But primarily I'm interested in finding out why three people have been killed."

"Three?"

"Gretchen Crane, Lawrence B. Reeves, and Jermaine Lister."

"Jermaine who?"

"Lister."

I watched her face. She showed no sign that the name meant anything to her.

"I don't know anyone named Lister," she said.

I didn't say anything. I should confront her with the identity of her girlfriend and see what she did with it. But I thought about Natalie sitting on the bench by the Charles River crying. Sometimes I wondered if I was tough enough for this business.

"Could you tell me how you met Natalie?" I said.

"I certainly cannot."

"Did Natalie know Gretchen?"

"I have nothing to say to you," Mary Lou said.

"What was Natalie's name when you met her?"

Mary Lou folded her arms and sat without speaking.

"Did she know about you and Lawrence B.?"

Mary Lou rose without a word and walked out of her office and down a short hallway and disappeared. I thought about following. But I figured she had locked herself in the lavatory and the thought of me pounding on the lavatory door was not an encouraging one. Nor did it seem like it would lead to a break-through in the case.

Over the next several days, I tried talking to the staff of Great Strides. It took longer than it should have because I had to do so without Mary Lou catching me, so I was forced to catch the women when they left the office on coffee break, or to eat lunch, or, *eek,* to smoke. Nobody knew anything about Natalie, about Gretchen's love life, about Lawrence B. Reeves, about Mary Lou's love life, about Jermaine Lister, or Tony Marcus, or what time it was. One young woman admitted early that Mary Lou had warned them against speaking to me. But I kept on until I had talked with everyone and learned nothing. The more recalcitrant the case became, the more stubborn I got. But after three days I was no closer than I had been, so I took Rosie and went to have dinner with Spike. Sometimes he had a good idea. Sometimes he was consoling. And even if he was neither, he was usually fun.

CHAPTER

53

WE WERE AT the best table in his restaurant with a bottle of gewürztraminer, having pasta and lobster tossed in a reduction of vodka and cream. Rosie had her own chair but spent most of the time on the floor under her chair with a soup bone. Spike had filled the marrow cavity with peanut butter and Rosie was single-minded and noisy in her determination to get all of it.

As we ate, one of the waitresses came over and spoke to Spike. "There's a gentleman at table four says he wants to speak with the manager."

"Sure," Spike said. "Excuse me, Sunny."

He walked to the gentleman at table four.

"You called?" Spike said.

"You the manager?"

"Yes, I am."

"Are dogs allowed in this restaurant?"

"Dogs?" Spike said. "You see a dog in here?"

"Right under the chair where you were sitting," the gentleman said.

"Then probably the answer to your question would be *Yes they are,* wouldn't it?"

The man was with a woman and another couple. They all looked at one another.

"Well," said the woman, "I can't believe that's sanitary."

Spike smiled courteously.

"If you saw the kitchen," he said, "you wouldn't worry about the dog."

The four people at the table stared at him. Spike continued to smile.

Then the man who'd questioned Rosie in the first place said, "Well...for crissake... I guess you'd better bring me the check."

"Certainly, sir."

Spike snapped his fingers, gestured to the waitress. She grinned and brought the check, and Spike came back to the table. Rosie's tail thumped as he sat down, but she didn't let up on the soup bone.

"They'll leave a big tip," Spike said.

"A tip?"

"Sure. It's not the waitress's fault that the manager is a prick. They don't want to be thought of as stiffs."

"So you think they'll tip her?"

"Too much," Spike said. "You hear anything from Elizabeth's former boyfriend, whatsisname?"

"The loathsome Mort? No."

"And the fabulous Mary Lou Goddard?" Spike said.

He was monochromatic tonight. Black suit,

black shirt, charcoal silk tie, gleaming black tasseled loafers.

"I'm having a little trouble bringing that to closure," I said. "I'm flattered, by the way, that you dressed up for me."

"My pleasure," Spike said. "If I was straight, I'd be on you like a terrier on a rat."

"And such a beautiful way with metaphor," I said.

"It's a simile," Spike said. "Tell me about Mary Lou."

I told him what I knew.

"Speaking of terriers and rats," Spike said.

"I want to know what happened."

"You could print that on your business cards." Spike deepened his voice. "Sunny Randall, Investigations: I Want to Know What Happened."

"Well, I do."

"It's one of your greatest charms, Sunny. Nothing too elevated, like the search for truth, or a passion for justice. You'll hang in on a case until the hinges of hell start to ice up, because you *want to know what happened.*"

"And, right now, I don't know what happened. And I don't know how to find out."

"Well, you know that there's a connection between Natalie and Gretchen and Mary Lou. And you know there's a connection between Jermaine, Natalie, and Tony."

"Yes."

"You've had no luck with Mary Lou."

"No."

"You've had no luck with Natalie."

"No."

"Gretchen and Jermaine are dead."

"Yes."

"Who does that leave you?"

"Tony."

"See, you knew it all along."

The anti-dog party left. The waitress picked up the credit card slip and brought it over to Spike and showed it to him.

"Twenty-five percent," Spike said to me.

"You know your clientele," I said. "My problem with Tony Marcus is how I get at him."

"You could go ask him."

"Would he tell me anything?"

"Of course not."

"So how do I get at him?"

"If I was sleeping with Richie Burke—and I wish I were—I'd see if I could could enlist him and his father and uncle."

"Why would Tony talk to me if they helped me?"

"I don't know, see what they can come up with. If you go in with the Burkes, at least, Tony's less likely to have you put to death."

"The Burkes already have a couple of men keeping an eye on me," I said.

"Buster and Colley," Spike said. "They could protect you from the likes of Jermaine, okay. But Tony wants you dead, Ty-Bop will shoot them and you before they can get their iron cleared."

"How do you know Buster and Colley?"

Spike smiled.

"How'd you know they were following me around?"

Spike smiled again.

"How do you know Ty-Bop?"

Spike kept his smile.

"You and Mona Lisa," I said. "But I don't want to ask Richie or his family for help."

"We been through this before," Spike said. "You love Richie?"

"Yes."

"He love you?"

"Yes."

"Well, one of the things love means is you help each other."

"I know."

"Richie wanted help, would you help him?"

"Yes. But to ask him to ask his family?"

"Richie asked you to help his uncle, would you do it?"

"Felix?"

"Yeah, Felix."

"If Richie asked me."

Spike leaned back in his chair and tented his fingers in front of his chin and smiled at me.

"God, you're smug," I said.

"With good reason," Spike said.

"If I am going to find out what happened...," I said.

"You're going to have to go through Tony," Spike said.

"And if I am going to go through Tony and survive..."

"You're going to need the Burkes," Spike said.

We listened to Rosie work on the bone for a while.

"You're right," I said.

"If there's a meeting and they want a public place on neutral ground, you can meet here."

"Thank you," I said.

"You're welcome."

CHAPTER

54

WE DIDN'T MEET at Spike's place. We gathered at one of the picnic tables set up on the rim of the parking lot at a rest area on Route 3, south of Boston. I sat on one side with Richie's father. Tony Marcus sat across from us. At the next table were Richie and his Uncle Felix. Ty-Bop leaned on the fender of a Lincoln Town Car with his arms folded and jittered to the beat of a different drummer. Junior loomed motionless beside him. Both sides had brought some soldiers, white guys with the Burkes, black guys with Marcus, and they sat, motors idling, in the parking lot. I could see Buster and Colley in one car.

Tony smiled at me.

"For a pretty little girl," he said, "you do stir things around."

This didn't seem the right time to explain to him that I was a woman, not a girl, so I smiled back at him.

"Just doing my job," I said.

"So, Desmond," Tony said to Richie's father, "what can I do for you?"

Desmond Burke had one of those ascetic Irish faces you see staring out of old IRA photographs. In another time he probably would have sought martyrdom at the barricades. He sat with his chin resting on his folded hands.

"As you might know, Tony, Sunny is like a daughter to me."

"Phil Randall know about this?"

In his own way Desmond Burke was a zealot, and like most zealots, he was humorless.

"So, if she's having a problem, I take it to be my problem as well."

"Nothing like a loving family," Tony said.

I glanced around. At the next table Felix Burke was paying no attention to us. He sat and stared at Ty-Bop. Felix was Desmond's younger brother, a thick-bodied man with sloped shoulders, a former boxer with scar tissue that narrowed his eyes and thickened his nose. Desmond was the theoretician of the Burke enterprise. Felix ran the implementation. I looked at Ty-Bop. He wasn't looking at us, either. He was watching Felix. Richie was watching me. When I looked at him, he winked.

"I don't much like it that Sunny wants to be a detective," Desmond said. "But Sunny don't seem much to care a damn whether I like it or not. She wants to be a detective, so she is."

"Broads do that," Tony said.

I imagined Mary Lou Goddard listening to this conversation.

"Now, Sunny needs some help from you, and she figures she goes at you by herself, you might get annoyed and have the jitterbug over there put her down."

If Ty-Bop heard himself called a jitterbug, he didn't react. Maybe Ty-Bop didn't listen to anything but gunfire.

"Sunny," Tony said, "you think I'd do that?"

"Of course you would," I said.

Desmond smiled. His smile was only facial. It was as if he knew when he was supposed to smile and he did so the way someone does for a photograph. The smile didn't linger and when it disappeared it left no trace.

"So I thought we might sit down and work out some sort of agreement," Desmond said.

He glanced back toward one of the cars idling near us, and raised his voice.

"Colley," he said, "bring me that thermos."

Colley got out of the car carrying a tall green thermos bottle with a silver cap that doubled as a cup.

"I took the liberty of bringing some coffee," Desmond said. "You want some?"

Tony shook his head. Desmond didn't offer it to anyone else. Colley unscrewed the cup carefully, took off the inner cap, and poured the coffee into the cup. Desmond nodded.

"Leave it," he said.

Colley set the thermos down and went back to the car. There was tension in his movements. Desmond picked up the cup with both hands and sipped at the coffee.

"What kind of agreement," Tony said.

If he felt any tension, he didn't show it. He seemed entirely relaxed, a pleasant man sitting at a picnic table with a few friends. Around us, closer to the building where the rest rooms were, tourists in bad-looking shorts and colorful tops carrying cameras and children embarked and disembarked, but they were inconsequential to this event, evanescent in the ordinariness of their comings and goings.

"Sunny's investigating a couple killings," Desmond said. "She says the investigation might stray over into your turf."

Tony didn't say anything. He didn't seem afraid of Desmond. Though Desmond was easy to be afraid of. In fact Tony never seemed afraid of anything. Which is probably how he got to be who he was.

"If it did," Desmond said, "we don't want you to clip her."

Tony grinned.

"Direct," Tony said. "Always liked that about you, Des, you're direct."

"Fact, we'd appreciate it if you helped her."

"Even if it's not in my interest?" Tony said.

I noticed that most of the black sound disappeared from his voice as he talked with Desmond.

"Sunny will keep you out of it."

"How do I know I can trust her?"

"You can trust me," Desmond said.

"And saying she does drift into my yard, and

260

say I don't like it, why shouldn't I put her down?"

"Because we been coexisting nice in this town and we wouldn't want that to change."

"You'd go to war over this little broad?" Tony said.

"Family," Desmond said.

He held his coffee in both hands, with his elbows resting on the tabletop, and tilted the cup slightly to drink. His eyes were very deep-set and he looked steadily at Tony over the rim of the cup. Tony leaned back a little on his side of the table, resting his hands palms down on the tabletop. He drummed his fingers lightly.

"I notice you've got a couple of hooligans following her around."

I felt a small clench in the center of my stomach. Tony had been keeping track of me.

"Two fine Irish lads," Desmond said.

Tony drummed on the table some more.

"It would make doing business harder, if we had to slug it out with you at the same time."

"It would," Desmond said.

Tony drummed some more.

"I make no promises," he said. "But if Sunny wants to come see me tomorrow, she comes alone, no flounder-belly Irish goons trailing after her, we'll talk and nothing will happen to her. After that it's one day at a time."

Desmond looked at me. I nodded. Richie was looking at Tony Marcus.

"If something happens to Sunny," Richie said, "you're dead."

Felix didn't seem to move but somehow I could see him focus more closely on Ty-Bop. I thought that Ty-Bop became a little stiller. Richie's stare could make doorknobs fall off. It was the part of him I never fully understood, nor ever fully liked. But if it bothered Tony, he mastered his emotions. Tony smiled.

"We're all dead sooner or later," Tony said.

"Sooner," Richie said.

CHAPTER

55

I WAS GOING to see Tony Marcus in the morning and I was thinking about it. A gun wouldn't do me much good if things went bad, but no matter, it would make me feel better to have one. Or two. I got out a two-shot .38 derringer from the closet where I locked up my guns, and experimented with where to conceal it on my person, until the phone rang. It was Elizabeth.

"I signed the papers," she said when I answered the phone.

"Elizabeth?"

"Of course. I signed his fucking papers for him."

"Divorce papers," I said.

"Naturally."

"That seems wise," I said.

"And I just wanted you to know that I'm going out on the town to celebrate."

"Good idea."

"And I've got a date."

I was completely insincere.

"Really?" I said. "Tell me about him."

"His name is Harvey. I haven't met him yet, but he's supposed to be fabulously wealthy."

"How'd you come to date him?"

"Well, I decided that it was time to stop sitting passively by, so I took steps."

"Such as?"

Elizabeth's voice got that defiant sound it got when she'd done something that embarrassed her and she didn't want to admit it.

"I took out an ad in the Personals column."

"And Harvey responded?"

"Yes."

"Was it from him you learned of his fabulous wealth?"

"Are we just a little jealous?" Elizabeth said.

"Where are you going to meet him?"

"Steak-O-Rama in Braintree."

In a shopping center off Route 3. Where all the multimillionaires hung out.

"Do me a favor?"

"What?"

"Meet him there and leave him there. Don't let him know where you live and don't be alone with him until you get to know him."

"You think he might be dangerous?"

"I don't know that he isn't," I said. "But it does no harm to let the relationship develop."

"I really do think you're jealous. Just a teensy bit?"

"Sisterly concern," I said.

"Well, just remember I'm not a little girl. Certainly you know I can take care of myself."

Just like you did with Mort.

264

"Sure," I said. "Have a nice time."

After I hung up, I looked down my loft at Rosie sleeping on her back on my bed.

"Thank God," I said to her, "you're not a jerk."

I tried the derringer in my bra. It was too heavy, it interfered with the bra's primary duty, and it made me look like I was carrying a concealed unicorn. I put on a big, loose thigh-length sport jacket with big pockets and tried that. No good. I didn't want to rummage about in so big a pocket if I needed the gun. My phone rang again.

"Please don't be Elizabeth," I said to the phone.

It wasn't. It was Julie.

"I TALKED WITH Michael," Julie said.

"And?"

"It was awful but it was important too. He's so angry. But he's so decent."

"What did you talk about?" I said.

"Us."

"I sort of guessed that," I said. "What about 'us'?"

"We are going to get some therapy."

"Separately?"

"Yes. Couples therapy is about solving the relationship. I need to solve myself and so does Michael."

"What do you think Michael has to solve?"

"That's up to Michael and his shrink," Julie said. "If I were them, I'd certainly want to examine why Michael has accepted my acting-out behavior for so long."

"And you?"

I could hear a rueful smile in Julie's voice.

"I'd examine why I've been acting out for so long."

"How does Michael feel about therapy?" I said. "He doesn't seem the type."

"No he isn't. But he's smart. And I think he can do it, if he's brave enough."

"Is he doing this in hopes of saving the marriage?"

"Oh, I'm sure he is. But psychotherapy goes where it will go, and what you think you're after at the beginning may not in fact be what you want later on."

"True," I said.

"So," Julie said, "are you proud of me?"

"Sure," I said. "This seems like progress. Are you still seeing Robert?"

"I'm not seeing anyone for the time being, until I get myself straightened out. Dating can serve as a sort of anodyne. I need to come to be able to be alone, before I can be with anyone."

"Well, I feel good about this," I said. "This is going to work out. I don't know how. I don't know if you and Michael will be together or apart. But I know either way you're both going to be fine."

"You really think so?"

"Absolutely."

At least sort of absolutely.

After we hung up, I went back to thinking about my visit to Tony Marcus, and Junior. And Ty-Bop. Was I scared? Yes. I guessed I was. It was so not a useful feeling that I kept it tamped down. But if I turned and looked straight at it, yes, I was scared.

"Why," I said to Rosie, "do you suppose that no one's calling up and saying 'How are you, Sunny? Are you scared? Do you have something bad to do tomorrow? Are you okay? Can I do anything?' Why do you suppose that is, Rosie?"

Rosie squirmed around a little on the bed, still on her back, and let her head loll toward me so that her black oval eyes were looking right at me.

"Yes," I said. "That's right. We had a little spurt of self-pity there. I'll try not to do it too much."

I undressed and put on my pj's and took off my face and washed. Then I loaded my short Smith & Wesson, and put two bullets into the derringer, and laid them side by side on my night table, and went to bed.

CHAPTER

57

I WAS WEARING ease-of-movement clothes—
jeans, a tee shirt, and sneakers—when I went
into Buddy's Fox, where Tony Marcus kept
his office. I had the .38 in my belly pack, and
the derringer in an ankle holster. The booths
along the right wall were maybe half full of
people having eggs and home fries. Junior
loomed on a bar stool, leaning back against
the bar, with his elbows resting on the bar top.
Ty-Bop stood beside him eating peanuts and
bouncing on his toes to the sound of something
he was listening to on headphones. Both
looked at me as I came in. Neither said anything. I was the only white person in the
place. I felt exposed and inappropriate.

The bartender was setting up for the day and
when he saw me, he nodded toward the narrow
hallway to the right of the bar. I walked past
the booths and down the short hallway and
knocked on the door at the end.

"Come in."

I turned the knob and went in.

Tony was sitting in a high-backed red

leather swivel chair at a big old mission oak table. The table had a phone on it, and a blank yellow legal-sized pad, and a Bic pen, and nothing else. Neither Junior nor Ty-Bop followed me.

"Shut the door," Tony said.

He was wearing a black suit with a wide chalk stripe, a white shirt, and a shimmering orange silk tie.

I shut the door. Tony got up and came around his table.

"I have to know if you're wearing a wire," Tony said.

I stood and turned my back to him and held my hands out away from my sides. Tony ran his hands over me without copping any more feel than he had to. If he discovered the ankle holster he didn't say so.

"Lemme see the belly pack," Tony said.

I unstrapped it and handed it to him. He unzipped it, took my gun out, looked inside, put the gun back in, zipped the belly pack back up, and handed it to me.

"Sit," Tony said.

I sat in a straight-backed mission oak chair.

"Anything I say in here," Tony said, "I'll deny outside of here. You understand?"

"Yes."

"What do you want to know?"

"Did you have Jermaine Lister killed?" I said.

Tony smiled.

"Sunny Randall," he said and shook his head slowly. "It's what I like about you. You don't fuck around."

"Did you?"

"Sure."

"Why?"

"He made a run at you."

"Without your approval?"

"Hell, without my knowledge."

"And you like me so much you had him killed?" I said.

"I do like you that much," Tony said. "But I had him killed 'cause he was a loose fucking cannon, and I wanted him quiet."

"About what?"

"About everything you want to know," Tony said. "It's why I'm talking to you. I figure maybe you get your curiosity satisfied, you'll stop fucking with this case."

"Why not kill me?"

"I keep telling you," Tony said. "I like you, Sunny Randall."

"And I'm harder to kill than Jermaine because nobody gives much of a damn about him, but the Burkes would take an interest in me."

"Burkes' interest weighs a lot," Tony said. "Don't scare me. I didn't get to be who I am by letting people scare me. But I didn't get here by wasting my time shooting it out with the Burkes either."

I made a little *doesn't-matter-which* gesture with my left hand.

"Tell me about Natalie Marcus," I said.

Tony let his chair rock back so his feet cleared the floor. He looked at the shine on his glistening black shoes for a moment.

"What you want to know?"

"You know her."

"Yes."

"Did you know her real name was Verna Lee and she was Jermaine's sister?"

"Yes."

"Did you know she was married to you at one time? When she was known as Natalie Marcus?"

Tony smiled, though I didn't see much warmth in the smile. But I never saw much warmth in Tony. He was playful. But what he really felt, or thought, or needed was never clear.

"I did know that," Tony said.

"Did you know she was once a hooker?"

"Um hm."

"Did you know she is now in a relationship with a woman named Mary Lou Goddard?"

"Sunny Randall," Tony said. "They going to take you to Sweden, give you the Nobel Prize in snooping."

"Did you know somebody named Lawrence B. Reeves?"

"Not sure," Tony said. "What about him?"

"He used to date Mary Lou Goddard, who's the current partner of your ex-wife. He used to employ the services of Natalie's brother, one of your pimps, Jermaine Lister."

"Ah," Tony said. "That Lawrence B. Reeves."

"Lawrence is dead. So is a woman named Gretchen Crane. Did you know her?"

Tony rocked slowly in his leather chair. He rubbed his eyes with the thumb and forefinger of his left hand, as if he were tired. He pursed his lips slightly. I never knew if Tony did anything spontaneously or if everything was for careful effect. I waited. He rocked.

Finally, he said, "Why you want to know all this, Sunny Randall?"

"Because I don't know it," I said.

"Simple as that?"

"It's what I do. I try to find out stuff. I like the work."

"You still got that funny-looking little dog?"

"I still have the beauteous Rosie," I said.

Tony nodded as if that somehow explained everything. He stopped rubbing his eyes, and with his chair still tilted back and his elbows resting on the arms of the chair, he folded his hands across the top of his stomach.

"Let me tell you a story," he said.

He moved his clasped hands up so that they were pressed against his lips.

"I got no regard for whores," he said. "They just product to me. Then about ten years ago, I met Verna Lee Lister. Just another whore, probably no different than any of the others. But I thought she was different."

Tony rocked forward and took a long narrow cigar from a humidor on his desk.

"Mind if I smoke?" he said.

"Yes."

Tony smiled and carefully lit the cigar, turning it until he had it burning evenly.

"I took her off the streets. I cleaned her up. I got her good clothes. Changed her name. Taught her table manners. Sent her to college.

We were going to boogie off into the sunset together."

"Pygmalion," I said.

"Don't know nothing about pig whatsis," Tony said. "But I thought it was going to be different."

"And it wasn't?"

Tony smiled without any sign of happiness, and inhaled cigar smoke. As he spoke the smoke drifted out between his words.

"It was, but not the way I thought. We were married awhile and then she takes up with a lesbian."

"Mary Lou Goddard?"

Tony nodded.

I heard myself say, "How did you feel about that?"

"How you think?" Tony said.

"Stupid question," I said. "What I meant was how did you feel about the lesbian part?"

"I tole her she do what she have to do, but don't embarrass me."

"By admitting she was a lesbian?"

"By admitting she left me for a dyke," Tony said.

"Ahhh," I said.

Tony nodded silently.

"In my position, don't do me no good to get laughed at," he said.

"Did Jermaine know?"

"Yes."

"And he exploited it," I said.

"It helped him get ahead in the organization," Tony said.

"Which is why he tried to kill me," I said. "If I found out about Natalie, he had no hold on you. His career would be over."

"And his life."

"Which as it turned out was the result of his efforts anyway."

"Things don't always work out," Tony said.

"Did you kill Gretchen Crane?" I said.

"Nope."

"Do you know who did?"

"The dyke," Tony said.

"Mary Lou?"

Tony nodded.

"Because she was having an affair with Natalie?"

"Yeah."

"And Mary Lou found out and killed her."

"Um hm."

"How do you know?"

"Natalie told me, wanted me to fix it."

"My God," I said. "Lawrence B. Reeves."

"He been following Mary Lou. Fact is he'd been fucking Mary Lou, or so Natalie says, which is why Natalie was fucking Gretchen whatsis, she says. 'Course Natalie can always come up with some good-sounding explanation, why she fucking some broad."

Except for anger, Tony had no other way to deal with his hurt.

"So you killed a couple of birds with one stone," I said. "You set him up for killing Gretchen and you stopped him from following Mary Lou."

"Un huh. Junior force him to sign the confession, didn't even have to touch him, Junior says. Reeves so scared he do whatever he was told. Probably shoot himself, they told him to."

"But he didn't shoot himself."

"No." Tony smiled. "Ty-Bop done that."

"I would have thought," I said, "that Natalie would have wanted Mary Lou to be punished for killing Gretchen. I mean they were lovers."

"Natalie tole me she felt bad for Mary Lou. Mary Lou saying 'Look what you made me do' and shit," Tony said.

"And Natalie felt guilty."

"She felt something," Tony said. "Mary Lou got the jingle. She pay for the place on Beacon Hill. She pay for the clothes and the lunches and the vacations to Truro. Only way Natalie know how to support herself is blow jobs."

"And Mary Lou had hired me to protect her from Lawrence B. before she found out about Natalie and Gretchen. And then when she'd killed Gretchen she had to get me out of her life before I found out."

"Smart girl," Tony said.

"Was it Natalie who got Gretchen access to the whores and Jermaine?"

"Through me."

"So why'd she go to Bobby Franco," I said.

"Natalie want a cop to know we doing business," Tony said. "She feel a little safer that way."

"And why in God's name would you have sent me to Jermaine, if you didn't want this stuff revealed?"

Tony held his cigar up so he could examine the burning end.

"That a mistake," he said. "I don't know why I done that. Sometimes I just do shit."

"If it all came out," I said, "it wouldn't hang over your head anymore."

"You a shrink too, Sunny Randall?"

"You still love her, don't you?"

Tony shook his head.

"Ain't part of the discussion."

Tony didn't seem to want to hear my theories of love, anger, and ambivalence. In truth I didn't either. I let it go.

"Is there anything to the fact that Lawrence B. did business with Jermaine every Thursday night?"

Tony snorted.

"Did he. Well, you use a whore in this city, you going to do business with one of my pimps."

"Just a coincidence."

"Far as I know," Tony said.

We were quiet. Tony smoked his cigar. I was sure there were loose ends I had missed. I was sure there were questions I would wish I'd asked. But right now, as far as I could think around the buzzing in my brain, I had it all.

"I'm going to try to prove as much of this as I can," I said.

Tony nodded. There was nothing playful about him.

"You can't prove anything without me."

"Just want you to know I'm going to try."

Tony rested his dark brown gaze on me.

"This gets to be a public thing, Sunny Randall, and fuck the Burkes, I'll have Ty-Bop shoot you dead."

I took a breath and pushed myself to say what I had to say.

"If I can prove you killed two people it'll be public, and I'll take my chances. But I won't gossip. Unless I can put you in jail I won't talk about what you've told me."

"Hope it works out that way, Sunny Randall," Tony said gently. "I'd kind of miss you."

Ambivalence writ large. I stood. We looked at each other and I left. I walked past Junior and Ty-Bop and the people eating breakfast and out into the sunlight.

CHAPTER

58

My CAR WAS parked across the street. And
as I walked to it, Spike stepped out of a
doorway and walked to meet me. As I reached
my car, Richie opened the door of a car across
the street and walked over. Spike and he
stared at each other.

"I was supposed to come alone," I said.

"Can't always have what you want," Spike
said.

"Did you two collaborate on this?" I said to
Richie.

Richie smiled.

"I didn't know he'd be here," he said.

I looked at Spike. He shrugged.

"I didn't know Richie would be here," he said.

"So the two of you, each on his own, came
down here."

"I guess so," Richie said.

"And hung around outside in case I needed
help."

Spike shrugged. I stared at both of them and
began to cry harder than I may have ever
cried in my life.